NIX & SCOTLYN:

THE WEDDING

(CUSTOM CULTURE, #5)

TESS OLIVER

NIX & SCOTLYN: THE WEDDING
Copyright © 2014 by Tess Oliver
ISBN-13: 978-1505435665
ISBN-10:1505435668

This book is a work of fiction. The names, characters, places, and incidents are products of the writer's imagination or have been used fictitiously and are not to be construed as real. Any resemblance to persons, living or dead, actual events, locale or organizations is entirely coincidental.

All Rights Are Reserved. No part of this book may be used or reproduced in any manner whatsoever without written permission, except in the case of brief quotations embodied in critical articles and reviews.

Prologue

Clutch was beaming as he lumbered toward me along the line of classic cars. "Just sold the El Camino for fifteen." The words shot out long before he reached me.

"Dude. Fifteen? Nice."

"Yep, and I've already got my eye on a sweet little '69 Camaro that just needs some love and she'll be a beauty." Clutch put his giant hand on my shoulder. "If only our high school classmates could see us now, especially the ones who started the betting pool that neither of us would graduate. I'm dipping in five digit car deals, and Nix Pierce, better known in the hallways of Chapman High as the Heartbreak Kid, just finished his first booked solid week of tattoos at his very own shop. Freefall is going to be the go to place for ink, you wait and see."

"Yeah, blows my mind how well the shop is doing. I finally hired someone full-time. Her name is Cassie, and she's fucking brilliant. I got really lucky."

"Was she that cute little, brainy-looking Goth girl with the piercings and the black rimmed glasses?"

"Oh, that's right, you were leaving when she came in for her interview. She is sharp. I will have to treat her like gold to make sure she sticks around." Someone fired up a crisp, loud set of speakers from a nearby truck. "I thought there was going to be a band tonight. There's a big enough crowd for it."

"I heard they canceled. But at least the food trucks are here."

I smiled up at him. I was six-two, but Clutch stood a good four inches over me, with a shoulder width to match his height. His super human size had earned him the nickname Viking, and it didn't hurt with the girls either. Keeping him fed was an all day event.

Clutch pulled a hundred dollar bill out of his wallet. "Taco truck? My treat."

I leaned closer and dropped my voice. "Shit, do you have fifteen grand in that thing?"

"Yeah, did you forget the earlier conversation? I sold the El Camino."

"I remember. I just didn't realize you got cash for it. I guess it's a good thing you are a human fortress. Just don't drop that thing in your quest to shovel in your usual dozen tacos."

Clutch glanced over the heads of the crowd and something caught his eye. "Speaking of high school, there's a circle of curious onlookers gathering over there. Must either be an argument or a spectacular car." He looked over at me. "Remember that day when those two chicks got into it in the lunch quad? We all circled around and got really quiet so as not to alert any of the proctors. One of the girls was that head cheerleader, Mandy, who you banged after prom even though she wasn't your date."

"And we're reminiscing about this because…"

He shrugged. "Don't know. The circle of people just reminded me of a fight." I couldn't see across the crowd and maze of cars as well as him. He glanced that direction again. "Yep, definitely a fight of some kind." And with those words, we both looked wide-eyed at each other.

"Damnit." I looked quickly around.

"Where the hell is he?" Clutch asked.

"He was sitting over there at that bench making the moves on some blonde in a short green dress and sandals."

Clutch sighed. "Did she have a sleeve of tattoos on her right arm?"

"Yeah."

Clutch started across the lot, and I followed, having to take extra long strides to keep up with him. "Remember that grumpy ass guy, Olson, with the sixty-six Nova and the build of a grizzly bear? The guy who was trying to tell me that I painted the El Camino the wrong shade of red?" We slid through the crowd, which grew denser as we neared the circle.

I knew where this was going. "Let me guess. The blonde Dray was hitting on is his girlfriend?"

"Yep."

We pushed through elbows and craning necks. Dray was standing in the center of the circle being held by two guys, who were considerably bigger than him, which wasn't saying much. Dray was small, but he was stronger and tougher than a goddamn gladiator. There were times I could swear he didn't feel physical pain, a survival skill he'd developed during a nightmarish childhood with a father who only knew how to communicate with his fist and belt. This seemed to be one of those times. A long stream of blood dripped from the corner of his mouth, and the side of his face was swollen. The half-bear, half-human asshole Clutch had mentioned drove his fist into Dray's gut just as we pushed into the center. The blonde stood nearby by pretending to look horrified, while, at the same time, basking in the knowledge that this was all because of her.

Dray sucked in the breath that had been knocked from him, and then a smile broke out on his face, causing the blood stream to thicken. "Hey, bros, look. This fool needs help from his two buddies to fight me."

The guy turned around to see who Dray was talking to. One of his eyes was swollen shut, and his lip was ripped open. And the idiot probably had no idea that Dray had obviously been holding back. Otherwise, the asshole would be face down on the ground trying to remember his name.

"Mason." He glared angrily at Clutch, which wasn't easy with one eye sealed shut. "It figures this little piece of shit is a friend of yours. You can watch while I pummel him into pudding." He spun around and drew back his arm, but Clutch grabbed hold of it. "What the fuck, Mason?" He tried to wrench his arm free from Clutch's iron grasp.

"Olson, if you want to fight him face to face, then go for it. You'll lose, but at least you'll be able to walk away with your balls. Three of you against one, that's just plain bullshit."

The crowd, the same group of people who'd been enthusiastically watching Dray get pinned and beaten, clapped wildly now throwing their support to the underdog. Although, Dray was rarely the underdog in any fight.

"Look what he did to my face," the guy sneered.

"An improvement if you ask me," Clutch said. The onlookers laughed. "Besides, you got off lucky. My friend here must have been feeling generous, otherwise, you'd be searching this asphalt for your fucking teeth right now."

Olson tensed his fist, and I wondered, for a second, if he was stupid enough to throw it at Clutch. He backed down. As I figured he would.

"Look, you got in your licks," I said. "This is over." I walked up to the guys holding Dray. "We're done here." They hesitated at first, but I didn't step away. They dropped their arms. I knew Dray well enough to anticipate what might come next. I stepped forward and put my hand on his shoulder before he took a swing at either guy. "Rosie's tacos will be sold out if we don't hurry." I also knew him well enough to know how to lure him away from fighting with his second favorite thing in the world— food.

With no more blood being splattered, the crowd slowly dispersed and headed back to the cars and the food. Olson and his two partners shot ugly scowls at us as the three of us walked past.

Halfway across the lot, Dray leaned over to spit out some blood. He wiped his mouth with the back of his hand. "Hey, Nix," he laughed, "I think you've got toilet paper on your shoe."

I bent over and lifted the paper off my toe. It was a flyer with a girl's picture. I smoothed it out. Clutch stared over my shoulder at the pin-up model. Her round blue eyes stared back at me as if she was asking my name.

I held the paper up to get a better look. "Holy shit."

Clutch glanced over at Dray. "Just exactly what are you using to wipe your ass with these days?"

Dray leaned over to look at the crumpled picture. "Jeez, she is something." He looked around. "I saw some girls dressed like pin-ups over by that Corvette earlier. Do you think she's here?"

"I was checking those girls out," Clutch said. "I would have remembered if I'd seen her."

They were having a conversation over my shoulder, but I couldn't drag my attention away from the picture. Besides being extremely beautiful, there was a layer of emotion in the girl's face. She was smiling, but it seemed to be a front. There was a touch of sadness in her crystal blue eyes.

Dray knuckled my arm. "Hey, tacos, remember?"

"Yep." I gazed at the photo a moment longer. Then I folded it and stuck it in my pocket.

Dray flashed me an obnoxious grin. "You're going to keep it?"

"Why would I throw out a picture of my future wife?" I asked.

Clutch laughed as he headed toward the taco truck.

Dray and I followed.

"Besides," I said, "I want to ask around and see if anyone knows her."

"Whatever floats your boat."

"Speaking of floating boats— you owe me your half of the rent. The marina raised the slip fee for the houseboat. So, pay up soon or we'll have to drift around at sea on the

Zany Lucy, and I'm not completely sure she's all that sea-worthy."

"Yeah, what gave it away? The puddle of ocean water under the kitchen table?"

"Just pay me soon."

"Yeah, yeah."

My phone rang. "It's my sister. Hey, go tell Clutch I want two carne asada and two chicken tacos. And remind him that he's treating."

I headed to the picnic tables as I answered the phone. "Hey, Diana, how did Nana's physical go?"

She paused.

"Di?"

"It went all right."

"What do you mean all right?"

"I mentioned to the doctor about how she seems to be forgetting stuff more and more and how she sometimes asks the same question a few minutes after she's already asked it."

"Yeah, I thought we figured it was just because she doesn't have Grandpa to talk to anymore." My grandmother had raised Diana and me after my dad, Nana's son, died in his race car, and my mom left us for her new life and lover. My dad's death had taken a huge toll on Nana, but she'd had us to take care of to keep her mind off the tragedy. Growing up, Dray and Clutch had spent more time at Nana's than with their own families. My wise and perfect grandmother had kept us all from going over the edge. We weren't the easiest trio of teenagers to manage either.

"The doctor wants to do a few tests to see if she's in the beginning stages of Alzheimer's," Diana's voice wavered.

"Shit. When are they going to start?"

"Next week. Can you take her?"

"I'll reschedule some stuff."

"Thanks. Well, I've got to feed the kids. I'll call you with the time and date tomorrow."

"All right. Hey, Di, the doctors are wrong. How could someone with as brilliant a mind as Professor Lucy Pierce have Alzheimer's? You know?"

"Doesn't seem possible to me either, Nix. But we need to prepare for whatever comes next."

"Yeah, all right. Talk to you later. Bye."

Clutch and Dray walked toward the table with the boxes of tacos and drinks. "Did this guy tell you about Barrett having to work thirty-six hour shifts on the fishing boat?" Dray asked as he lowered the food to the table. "Shit, there's only one thing I can imagine holding Rett's attention for that long, and it's got nothing to do with fishing."

"You look like you dropped your ice cream," Clutch said to me as they climbed over the bench. "Still thinking about that picture?"

I shook my head. "Diana called. Nana is going to go in for tests to see if she has Alzheimer's."

Clutch placed down the taco he was holding, and Dray put on that hardened mask that he used to hide emotion. My two friends loved my grandmother as much, or maybe even more, than their own parents.

"That sucks," Clutch said.

Dray pushed away the taco bag. "Can't eat these with a split lip anyhow."

I looked around at the people milling about the cars. "Life sure knows how to slap you around when you least expect it."

Chapter 1

Nix

Three years later.

I reached into the pocket of my shorts to make sure the small velvet box was still there. I was nervous as hell. The guy who everyone had called Heartbreak Kid in high school was nervous about a girl. But Scotlyn wasn't just any girl. She was *the* girl. There was no one else but her. I'd been in love with her since I'd found her picture, keeping it tucked in my wallet in what Dray had referred to as my ugly little slide into stalkerdom. The day the object of my obsession walked into Freefall, my life turned upside down. Haunted by a horrible tragedy, she could only communicate with notes and hand gestures. And so, armed with only a pen and paper, the girl, the complete stranger, who'd captured my heart with just her picture, scrawled herself right into my soul. I was so damn nuts about Scotlyn, two years later, she was still making my head spin.

I didn't bother to dress. I stepped into the tiny kitchen. Scotlyn stood at the sink sipping a glass of water. Her silky blonde hair cascaded over her tanned shoulders. She'd pulled back on her skimpy tank shirt but nothing else. The early summer sun had set leaving behind enough warmth that the galley on the Zany Lucy was bathed in drowsy heat. Hints of the triple digit California summer lurked just around the corner. It would be our last time on the boat. The Zany Lucy's new owners would be hauling her up north tomorrow for refurbishing.

Scotlyn turned. Her smile lit up the shadowy kitchen. We'd been together two years, but every time I looked at her, every time I touched her, it was like the first time. She could turn me to jelly with a simple gesture like pushing a strand of hair behind her ear.

"I'm going to miss seeing you on this boat." I pulled out a chair and sat down. The table was covered with wine glasses and snacks.

"I'm going to miss being here." Scotlyn had planned the evening, hoping it would make me feel better about having to sell off the boat named after Nana, my grandmother. My grandparents had lived on it in the early years of their marriage, and my grandfather had left it to me. Dray and I had lived on it for a long time, but I didn't have the money for the upkeep and the slip rental had increased so much I could no longer afford to keep her at the marina. The man who bought her happened to be married to a woman named Lucy, and so, they'd both decided it was fate and made a good offer. The money would help pay for Scotlyn's nursing school.

Scotlyn walked around the table and stood in front of me. I gazed at her. I had every curve memorized. It was impossible for me to be this close and not touch her. I reached out and took hold of her hips. We'd spent the last two hours drinking wine and making love, but I wanted her again.

A tiny wicked glint flashed in her big blue eyes. "Will

that chair hold both of us?"

"If it can hold Clutch, it can hold the two of us."

She tapped her chin with her finger in consideration for a second. "I guess we'll find out." She straddled my lap. My face pressed against her breasts as she slid slowly down over my cock. I slid her shirt up and ran my tongue along the edge of the scar that stretched from her breast to her hip. The vine of flowers, the tattoo that had brought her into my life, laced erotically around the pink scar.

The chair squeaked angrily and she giggled. I slid my hands underneath her naked ass, and she rose up and down over me. I lifted my face to hers. She lowered her lips to mine, driving her small tongue into my mouth as I filled her over and over again. Her movements quickened as she rocked her hips forward and ground her sweet pussy against me. Nearing climax, she pulled her lips from mine, and her head lulled back. Soft moans fell from her mouth, and she held tightly to me as her lithe, satiny body wriggled against me. I watched her amazing face as her wet pussy clenched around my cock. Still shuddering, she slid back and forth over me, bringing me to the edge. I held her tightly and moved against her, thrusting deep inside of her. A low groan rolled up from my throat, and I held her over me as I came.

She collapsed against me. "They just don't make chairs like this anymore," she sighed happily.

"Let's move this out to the couch. This well-made chair is starting to feel hard on my ass."

She stood and led me back to the main room, which was only slightly bigger than the kitchen. We climbed under the blanket Scotlyn had packed for our little celebration. My attention flitted to my shorts that were draped over the arm of the couch. I took a deep breath and reached for the box. My phone rang right then. I abandoned my plans to grab the box and glanced down at the screen.

"It's my sister," I said. "I'll call her later." Diana's ill-timed call had made my courage falter. I leaned back.

Scotlyn rested her head against my shoulder and brought the blanket under her chin. "Sometimes, when I'm sitting here with you like this, I have to assure myself that this is all real. You make me incredibly happy, Nix Pierce." She lifted her face and kissed my cheek.

That was my cue. I took a deep breath and reached for the box. She hadn't noticed it in my hand yet. "Scottie, please promise me that you'll be with me forever." I lifted the box up above the blanket and opened it. Her blue eyes rounded as she looked at the ring. I turned toward her. "Scotlyn James, will you marry me?"

Her mouth parted, and she gazed speechlessly at the ring. My phone rang again. I was crossing my sister off the wedding list.

Scotlyn looked at my phone with worry. "You need to answer it." Unfathomable hardship and heartbreak had given her an uncanny ability to sense trouble. I grabbed the phone. "Diana?"

"Nix," Diana sobbed. I knew what was coming next before the words even came through the phone. "Nana's gone."

Scotlyn read my expression, and her hands flew to her face.

"Diana, I'll call you back in a few." I couldn't keep the

waver out of my voice. I stuck the ring box back in my pocket and pulled Scotlyn into my arms.

CHAPTER 2

Scotlyn

Nana looked more fragile today than usual, but her eyes sparkled with a gleam I hadn't seen before. She was sitting propped up against her pillow. My usual chair had already been placed by her bedside. There were days when it took her a few moments to remember who I was. She'd only known me for just over a year. I wasn't one of the lucky people who had known her their whole life, but we'd grown extremely close in the short time. Nana had wanted her memoirs written in long hand, insisting every story turned out more interesting in handwriting. And my long years of silence had taught me to be an extremely fast writer.

Helping her write down her long, wonderful history before it was shredded away by her disease had helped me more than it had helped her. Her life story, complete with humor, adventure and plenty of heartbreak, had helped me face my own terrible tragedy. In her youth, Nana had been an academic, a left wing activist, what some might have called a radical. But to me, she had been part of the same culture as my parents. But while Nana's hardcore edge had softened as she grew older, my own parents had not had the chance to mellow with age.

"Come sit, Scotlyn." Her smile glowed as usual, but there was something behind it today. "We are not going to write memoirs today."

I placed the paper pad and pen on the nightstand.

"Oh, but you'll need that, my dear." The haze in her pale eyes grew more opaque each day. "My doctor says my heart is not going to last much longer."

I bit back tears and took hold of her hand. It was soft and mottled with age spots.

"No tears, please, my dear. You know, I consider myself lucky to go long before my memory is completely erased." She patted my hand. "Now, here's what I have in mind, and we must hurry because the drugs, the B-12 shot, and my enthusiasm for this have sharpened my mind today. I'm going to dictate a letter for you to read at my funeral."

My mouth dropped open. "Me?"

"Yes. And it won't all be sugar and roses."

I laughed. "A letter from you? No, I wouldn't expect sugar and roses."

"There will be plenty of heartfelt words, but I thought it might be fun to slap a few people from the grave. More effective, I think."

I smiled. "I might need a few shots of whiskey to deliver the letter, but if it's your wish, then I'm at your command."

"Wonderful. I know you can do it." Her smile always reminded me of warm tea and honey on a dreary day. "I can't think of a lovelier person to be my voice at my own funeral. Of course, that is, assuming people will show up to it." She laughed.

"I'm sure they will."

"I've told Diana what my wishes are, but perhaps, I should tell you too. My granddaughter sometimes has a hard time hearing over her own opinions."

I smiled. I'd only met Nix's sister a few times, but I'd already come to that conclusion about her.

"I want a gravesite funeral only, because I want to be by my husband and son's sides as quickly as possible. No in between baloney. And no open casket. Please don't let anyone see me dead. People never look their best when they're dead."

Nana was one of the few people who could make you want to cry and laugh in the same moment.

"Well, shall we get started?" she asked. "Scotlyn?"

"Scotlyn?" Cassie's voice pulled me out of my thoughts.

I stared down at the paper with Nana's letter. I'd written it in short hand to keep up with her words, which on that day had flowed quickly and with incredible alacrity, making it seem unfathomable to think the woman suffered from dementia. I'd rewritten the letter in large clear print to make sure I didn't stumble over any word, but my courage had waned once we got to the cemetery.

"How are you feeling?" Cassie knew about my trepidations of having to read something in front of a lot of people, many of whom were complete strangers. I'd only just found my ability to speak again a year and a half ago, and this was a daunting task for me. And having to read Nana's words without breaking down into sobs seemed near to impossible.

"I don't know if I can do this, Cassie. But at the same time, I can't let Nana down. She counted on me to be her voice at the funeral." My fingers shook as I folded the paper and pushed it inside my purse. I waved that same shaky hand in front of my face. "Why must it always be so darn hot in summer?"

Cassie smiled and wrapped her hand around my arm. "I could go into the whole seasons and moving closer to the sun science lecture, but I don't think you're in the mood. Look, Finley mentioned to me earlier that she knew some good breathing exercises if you needed them. I think you need them. She's over there under the tree with Taylor."

People were starting to gather along the rather treacherously steep hillside where Nana's funeral would take place. A half circle of chairs had been arranged in front of the freshly dug grave. Nana would be buried next to her husband and her son. The Hearst would be driving down from the funeral home in a few minutes. The guys were getting their pallbearer gloves and instructions. Most of the people were, as I expected, unfamiliar. Several of Nana's professor friends had traveled from the east coast, and a few of the nurses who had formed a special attachment to Nana had come too.

Cassie and I held hands as we climbed to the tree where Finley and Taylor had found shade from the midday sun. An older couple who seemed extraordinarily robust and tall with pure white hair, traveled slowly down the incline to the gravesite.

"Cassie, are those two people—"

"Clutch and Rett's parents? Yep. Easy to guess, huh?"

"Yep."

"Finley," Cassie said as we got to the tree, "Scottie needs some of those breathing exercises. She has to read

Nana's letter in front of everyone, and she's feeling a little anxious."

Finley's almond-shaped eyes peered up from under her long curtain of white bangs. "You've come to the right person." She tapped her chin, apparently flipping through her mental list of breathing techniques. "Yes, I think for a case like this we need to give you something you can do now and then again just before it's time to go up and read. It's call Breath Moving. Basically, you close your eyes and as you breathe imagine the oxygen flowing up to your head and then down to all your extremities, getting rid of any tingling or tremors. Think of that breath just filling your body and calming you down." Finley glanced around. "We can all do it."

We grabbed hands and formed a circle. "Now, close your eyes," Finley instructed. "Forget about everything around us, forget that we are standing in a cemetery. Transport yourself somewhere cool and quiet and dark." Finley spoke softly. "Now, take a deep, long breath and imagine that oxygen flowing through your body."

We performed Finley's breathing exercise for several minutes, and remarkably, I felt much less shaky. I was feeling better than I had in the last few days, when dealing with the reality of losing Nana had gone from shock to anger to profound heartbreak.

The loud, rumbling motor of Clutch's car sounded in the distance. It rolled down the stretch of road that led to the gravesite. The white Hearst followed at a snail's pace. Clutch parked, and the four of them climbed out of the car. They pulled on their white gloves and waited for the Hearst to stop. Nix looked pale and thin. He'd hardly eaten for the last few days. And for the last few nights, he'd hardly slept. If he wasn't tossing and turning, he was up pacing around the dark house. Aside from his dad, Nana had been the most important person in his life, and his sense of loss was palpable.

Still holding tightly to each other's hands, Cassie, Finley, Taylor and I walked down the hillside to where the others had gathered. Everyone watched as the Hearst parked at the curbside. A taxi pulled up several cars back, and a woman stepped out. She was dressed in a crisply tailored black suit and wore a wide brimmed black hat and sunglasses. Something about the way she carried herself reminded me of an old time movie star. She had trouble walking over the grass in her heels. She'd caught everyone's attention. Diana had been standing with her husband and two boys near the family chairs. Her mouth dropped open. She shot a look over at Nix. Cassie noticed Diana's reaction too.

I looked at her. "Do you think it's her?" I asked.

Nix's face was hard and his mouth was pulled tight as he strolled across the lawn to meet the woman. "I think that answers the question," Cassie said.

He gave her a brief, polite hug and helped her finish the long trek across the grass.

"Poor Nix." I hated seeing him in so much pain. "He looks like a lost little boy today." He led his mom toward us, and some of my nervous tremors returned. His mom was pretty, someone who'd lived the good life in Europe. A lack of wrinkles for someone her age. A woman who'd hardly taken the time to fret about her husband's death or leaving behind her kids.

The mixture of emotion in Nix's face made my throat

tighten. "Scotlyn, this is my mom, Katherine." With the swirl of emotion in his expression, came a tone that was as hard and cold as stone.

"How do you do, Scotlyn?" She glanced at me for a long moment. "You are as beautiful as the pictures I've seen." She turned to Nix. "Alex, sweetheart, can you help me over to Diana. I don't trust myself on this steep slope."

"Nice meeting you," I said quietly.

Taylor elbowed me. "Hey, your first meeting with the mother-in-law. Fun, huh? I'll bet you're glad she lives on the next continent."

Cassie leaned in. "Dray's mom is over there in the dark red dress and Florida suntan. She's a gem too. I guess it's only appropriate that all these people came to pay respects to the woman who took over when their parenting skills failed miserably." Cassie's sharp tongue never left out any of the obvious. It was part of why I loved her.

I smiled and thought briefly about the words mother-in-law. Nix had stunned me with a proposal just as the call came in from Diana. It was wretched having to forever match those two events together. It had felt like a bad omen, and my own unplanned reaction had also left a darkness in my heart. And I couldn't completely explain it to myself. I'd lost my entire family, and now, Nix was my only true family. I couldn't bear the thought of ever losing him. After losing my sister and parents, I'd promised myself I would never love anyone like I loved them. Then I would never have to suffer such unspeakable loss again. My attachment to Nix scared me to death.

So much had happened in the past few days, I was sure Nix had completely forgotten about the ring. It was for the best. "Oh no," I said suddenly, "Nana's letter. I didn't expect Nix's mom to show."

"Uh, let me guess," Cassie said. "The section about Nix's mom is not all that flattering?"

I looked at her.

"Maybe you could skip that part," Finley suggested.

I thought about that. "No, Nana told me she thought it would be fun to slap a few people from the grave."

The girls laughed.

"I am so bummed I never got to meet Nana," Finley said. "She sounds like my kind of person."

"Look," Taylor said, "they're opening the back doors of the Hearst."

Everyone stood and watched as Nana's small, pearl white casket was withdrawn from the Hearst. The guys were all dressed in suits and wearing the grimmest expressions I'd ever seen. My tears flowed in torrents, the second they took their designated spots along the casket. And I realized it wasn't just the thought that Nana was inside that pushed me to sobs, it was seeing Nix, Clutch and Dray carrying the woman who had held them in check, the woman who had saved all their butts from trouble, the woman any of them would have stepped in front of a train for. They were three of the toughest guys I knew, yet today under the blazing summer sun, looking awkward and uncomfortable in suits and ties, they looked lost and heartbroken.

Cassie's shoulders shook, and I placed my arm around her. Taylor came up next to me and took hold of my arm with shaky hands. She laid her head on my shoulder and tried futilely to keep up with wiping away the steady stream of tears on her face. We all three knew these guys better than anyone, anyone but Nana, of course, and now she was gone. It was going to leave a hole in all their hearts.

The chairs were meant for the family members, but we'd left them open for some of the older attendees. Once they'd performed their pallbearer duties, the four guys joined us. It seemed each of us couldn't get close enough to our prospective mates. I held tightly to Nix, my anchor, the solid part of my life, who if I lost, I would never recover. And he held me tightly too as if a sudden wind might sweep through at any moment and carry me away.

Nana was not a religious woman, and the sermon was sweet and simple, the way she would have liked it. Several friends got up to speak, but none of the guys thought they could hold it together enough to say anything. For the past few days they had been eulogizing her in their own unique way, just them and a lot of beer, at our kitchen table, Nana's kitchen table. The stories they told had us shifting between laughter and tears.

Finley's breathing exercises had worked for a few seconds, but when it was time for me to walk up and read Nana's letter, the rush of nerves returned.

Nix looked down at me. "Are you going to be all right?"

I took a deep breath. Nana had asked this of me, and I had to suck it up and do it. I wouldn't be able live with myself if I chickened out. I smiled and nodded. Nix kissed my forehead. Everyone seemed especially quiet as I walked up to the front.

I unfolded the paper and looked around at the sad faces. The girls were all flashing me the thumbs up, and a nervous laugh spurted from my mouth. Then, suddenly, as if Nana had decided to stand right next to me for support, I found my tongue and my courage.

"Hello, everyone. I'm Scotlyn. I'm Nix's girlfriend, and I was fortunate enough to spend a lot of time with Nana—" I cleared the tightness from my throat. "Or Lucy as some of you may remember her. For the past two years, I've been helping Nana write down her memoirs." I swallowed hard and took a deep breath. "I can't begin to tell you how special it made me feel to sit in on all her humorous, sad, wild and occasionally shocking stories. About six months ago, I walked into her room. She'd been told by the doctor that her heart wouldn't last much longer. She'd told me she thought the one lucky aspect of being terminally ill was that you had time to make amends, tell certain people how much you loved them and to blow off a little steam if needed." A low chuckle made its way through the crowd. I took another breath and forged on. "And so, I have a letter from Nana to read to all of you."

I unfurled the paper. I looked across the grass toward Nix for a shot of courage. His smile was all I needed. "First of all, I'd like to thank Scotlyn for reading this at my funeral. I would have liked to have read it myself but... well..." More quiet laughter. "I never would have considered any girl worthy of my dear little Alex, but I was utterly and completely wrong, Scotlyn. You are truly lovely." My throat seized up briefly. I swallowed away the dryness and forged on. "To Greta and Nancy, my two nurses, I just want to say thanks for putting up with me on grumpy days. I know I was a bear, and you two always smiled through it. Oh, and by the way, on the mornings when I'd adamantly insisted that I hadn't had my donut yet and you both humored me with another donut figuring I had just forgotten, it was a trick. I figured, what's the use of having dementia if you can't use it occasionally to get a second maple bar? Which brings me to my little shout out to the inventor of donuts— well done."

Laughter followed. The two nurses, in tears, hugged each other. "And to my dear old friends, Ruth and Terrence, shame on you both for outliving me, but let me say, I wouldn't have given up my days of knowing you both for anything. What, between our arrests for protesting the war, our unbreakable resolve in thinking that our opinions were the only ones that mattered and our week long celebration of the Nixon resignation...well, anyhow, it will all be in the book." More laughter, which made my task easier.

"To my dear loves, Richard and Alexander, when this is being read, I will be with you already, and I confess, knowing that makes death come much easier. We'll talk when I get there. Much to discuss." A laugh spurted from my lips. I remembered writing those words and the two of us had had a good laugh over them. "And to my amazing granddaughter, Diana—" Nix's sister sniffled loudly on the chair in front of me. I paused for her to compose herself. I knew Nana had wanted her to hear every word. "You helped fill a void left behind when your father died. You were my closest, dearest friend, and even though you had no good role model for motherhood, you are so perfect at it, and Jamie and Alec are wonderful. And speaking of role models— Katherine, if you actually showed up for my funeral then maybe you aren't as terrible as I thought." I spurted the words out, and I was sure I saw the woman with the big black hat fidget. I moved on quickly. "You did, after all, provide me with two amazing grandchildren, and for that, I thank you. Your loss was my gain."

"And now for the boys. Even though, by blood, I only had one true grandson, who I adore with all my heart, in reality, I was blessed with three grandsons." I took another breath. "Dray, my sweet, lovely, all too vulnerable, Dray. And I know that you'll cringe at those adjectives, but those are the words that come to mind when I think of you. My only true regret in life was that I didn't do more to help you. I'm sorry, sweet Dray, for that. But you know how much I loved you and that gives me some comfort." There had been laughter a few seconds before and now tissues were being dragged back out. I peered across the heads. Cassie was hugging Dray. He looked completely shaken, something totally out of character for Dray. I had to compose myself or I would never finish. "And Jimmy, or Clutch, as everyone calls you only I've never figured out why, you never needed me quite as much. You were born taking care of yourself. I always marveled at how strong and independent you were. I know you had no choice. I just remember how upset you were the day your father sent Barrett off to work on one of those dangerous crab boats. You pretended to be so mad at your brother for getting in trouble, but deep down, I knew you were sick with worry for him. I only hope your parents realize what an amazing and resilient person you are. Although, I fear they do not." Taylor was pressed tightly against Clutch's side. He'd kept his dark sunglasses on the entire day. I knew there were tears underneath, but I was just as glad not to see them now. "And Alex, the light of my life. Without you, I never would have recovered from your father's death. As far as I'm concerned, you can do no wrong. You are my light." I willed myself to look up at Nix. He was standing with Dray and Cassie and looking as lonely and sad as I'd ever seen him.

I folded the paper. There was a mixture of sorrow, humor and even a bit of humiliation in the faces around me. Which, it seemed, was exactly how Nana had planned it.

While friends and family drifted back to their cars, I stood with our friends as Nix walked his mother back to the taxi. They spoke for a few minutes and he gave her a brief hug before she climbed back into the cab. "She makes my mom look like fucking Mary Poppins," Dray commented as we watched Nix shut the door.

The pain on Nix's face was hard to look at as he trudged back toward us. He'd been so busy these past few days, I realized we'd hardly spoken and I missed him. I headed toward him, and his arms went out so I could tuck myself against him.

He pressed his mouth to my ear. "I love you, Scotlyn." They were words that comforted me and terrified me at the same time. I'd found someone who I cared so deeply for, my world would come apart if I ever lost him.

Chapter 3

Nix

It had been a long day, and I was glad to be done with my last tattoo. The shop had been crazy busy, so busy that I'd hired another full-time tattoo artist. She called herself Stormy, and her artwork just blew me away. I couldn't quite tell what Cassie thought of her yet. Cass could be standoffish until she figured a person out. Stormy, like her name, tended to walk in every morning like a tempest, loud, wild and wanting attention. I didn't mind, but I could tell Cassie wasn't thrilled. The fact that Dray had stupidly, but not uncharacteristically, made a comment about Stormy's smoking hot body probably hadn't helped.

Cassie sneezed as I stepped out to the front.

"Bless you. Are you getting sick?" I asked.

She shook her head and then leaned over to make sure Stormy was out of earshot. "It's her darn perfume." She wiped her nose with a tissue. "She must bathe in the stuff."

"I guess it's a little overwhelming."

"You think?"

"I'll mention it to her. Look, Cass, she's doing great work, and she brought in her own string of regular clients.

I was super lucky to get her in the shop." I leaned over and kissed her forehead. "Just like I was super duper lucky, not once, but twice, to hire you for the shop."

"God, your flattery is so shallow and see through. Super duper." She rolled her eyes behind her big glasses. "Dray is coming by to pick me up after he gets done at the gym. I can close up if you want to get out of here."

"Yeah, that'd be cool. I think Stormy is almost done back there. Scotlyn and I haven't really gone out since Nana died." I leaned on the counter. "Hey, Cass, has Scotlyn said anything to you about—" I stopped. The proposal had been stuck in my head since that night. Diana's call had wiped it away, but I'd hoped that Scotlyn would say something about it. She hadn't. "Nevermind."

"What?" she asked incredulously. "You can't start a conversation like that and not finish. I knew something was eating at you. Out with it." She stared up at me expectantly.

"On the night that we got the call about Nana, I had just proposed to Scotlyn."

Her hand flew to her mouth as a tiny squeal of joy shot out. She lifted her arms to give me a congratulatory hug, but I stopped her. "I mean *just* proposed. I popped the question as the phone rang."

She seemed to comprehend what I was saying. "You mean she never had time to answer?"

I shook my head. "And, of course, that was it. We were both so devastated by the call, we never brought it up again."

"But that's not what's bothering you." Cassie knew me so well it was almost scary.

"Her reaction as I showed her the ring—" I shook my head. "She looked kind of shocked."

"Well, that's normal, I think. I mean, if Dray put a ring in front of me, I'd probably faint."

"Yeah, I guess. But it wasn't a good 'oh my god I can't believe it' shock. It was pretty fucking disappointing, and then the call came and— and it just seemed that was the final blow to the whole idea. I mean, it's not exactly the kind of proposal a girl dreams about."

She reached forward and patted my arm. "Scotlyn was really broken up about losing Nana. And between work and school and homework, she's so busy. Why don't you call her right now and ask her on a date. Then, if it feels right, you can bring up the proposal again." She smiled at me. "Nix, when you walk into the room, I swear Scottie's feet float up off the ground. She is absolutely bonkers in love with you. You are stressing about nothing."

I hugged her. "Thanks, Cass. I think I'll call her right now." I headed around the corner and crashed right into Stormy. Or rather, she crashed into me...again. She tossed her head of red curls back and laughed but managed to stay pressed against me in the interval.

"Oops! That is the third damn time I've barreled into you this week."

I stepped back because she didn't seem inclined to.

"I never hear you coming. It's almost as if you float around with little wings on the backs of your shoes." She sidled past me. I glanced back at Cassie. Another eye roll. But Cass was right— too much perfume. I headed into my small, cluttered office and sat at my desk. I stared down at my phone a second. What I hadn't mentioned to Cassie was

TESS OLIVER

that since the proposal, it seemed that Scotlyn was pulling away from me some. When we'd met, Scotlyn and I had formed a deep connection almost instantly. And that connection had been unbreakable until now. She spent most of her spare time poring over her textbooks and doing homework. I knew she wanted to excel in school, and I was proud as hell of her, but lately, it seemed the work was an excuse not to spend time with me. At first, I blamed it on the shock of losing Nana. We'd both experienced our share of horrible loss, but hers had come all at once in a terrifying accident that had left her in such despair, she'd lost her ability to speak. The years that followed were almost as bad. When she was only sixteen, she ran away from an awful aunt, her only remaining family, and lived on the streets before falling under the care of a controlling man who was obsessed with keeping her as his possession. She'd come remarkably far and, with a good deal of therapy, she'd found her voice again. But now, I was convinced there was something else going on, and it bothered me plenty.

I picked up the phone and felt like a young kid making his first call to a girl. "Hey, baby, what are you doing?"

"I'm just heading to the campus library." Car motors and other people's conversations rumbled through the phone. "What's up?"

"Nothing much." I picked up the hole punch off my desk and squeezed it in my hand like one of those rubbery stress relievers. The tiny compartment on the bottom popped open and hundreds of paper dots covered my desk. "I was thinking of making some reservations at that little Italian restaurant you like so much. What do you say? You, me, red wine and some extremely mind-blowing sex afterwards."

A horn blasted through the phone, and I pulled it away from my ear for a second. "Sorry, everybody is in a hurry to get out of here tonight. Sweetie, can I get a rain check on dinner? I'm meeting my study group at the library. We're exchanging notes for finals."

I started flicking the paper dots off my desk with my finger. "I've got to work all day Saturday. Why don't you study then?" I wasn't sure what I hated more— that she couldn't make time for me or that I sounded like a complete ass begging for some attention.

"Cassie, Taylor and I are driving out to see Finley and Rett at their Sweet Haven Rescue Barn on Saturday. Cassie is taking pictures for a magazine article to drum up interest and donations."

I swept my hand through the pile of dots, and they fluttered across the room. "Great. I guess I'll talk to you later."

"Are you mad?"

"Nope," I said sharply, assuring her that I was. "I'll find something to do. Be careful walking through the parking lot tonight. Bye."

"I won't be too late," she blurted just before I hung up.

Dray was standing at the counter as I walked back out.

"Hey, bud, what's up?" Dray absently dragged his finger across the handmade earrings in Cassie's display, and she promptly slapped his hand away.

She didn't have to look long at me to know how her suggestion had gone. "No date, huh?"

Dray's attention snapped my way. "Date? With who?"

"Who the fuck do you think?" Dray could get on my nerves fast when I was in a bad mood. And I was definitely

35

that.

"Sorry, jeez, touchy tattoo artist." He clapped his hands together once. "But I've got good news. Tank's Gym is hosting an amateur fight this Saturday night. Another club on the other side of the valley was supposed to host, but they pulled out. I let Rett know. You should talk Clutch into coming. Maybe he can pull himself away from work for two seconds and have a little fun."

"Not sure if watching two guys pound each other is on the top of my fun list right now."

His mouth pulled tight. "Yeah, if you're going to be in this pissant mood on Saturday, then you should just stay home."

Cassie looked at both of us. "It's like watching two old curmudgeons trying to outgrump each other." She sighed. "Look, Nix, you're reading too much into all of this."

"Into what?" Dray asked, never knowing when to shut up.

"Nothing," Cassie cut him short. "Take me home, Dray. I'll make you an omelet."

"With cheddar cheese?" His mood was already lighter, but mine grew darker by the minute.

Cassie rolled her eyes. "Yes, with cheddar. We'll see if we can't get those arteries nice and clogged before you hit forty." She grabbed her sweater from the hook and glanced back at me. "Wasn't your sweatshirt on this hook earlier?"

"Yeah." I glanced around. "I must have moved it somewhere."

Dray raised his fist for a bump. "We cool?"

"Yeah, and I'll think about Saturday."

They walked out. I went into the back room to see if Stormy was close to finishing her last tattoo. She was hunched over the guy's leg in my sweatshirt. She had the extra long sleeves pushed up high over her elbows, displaying the vast array of tattoos that covered her right arm.

She smiled back at me. "Hey, boss, almost done here."

"Great, I'm just going to clean up while you finish."

I walked past her.

"I hope you don't mind I pulled on your sweatshirt. The air conditioner vent is right over this chair."

I nodded a hello at the guy on the table. "Yeah, in the summer this shop runs too cold. Not much I can do about it. If we turn off the air, it gets too stuffy."

"I'll remind myself to wear more clothes tomorrow." Stormy's wardrobe seemed to consist mostly of extra-mini skirts and leather halter tops and, apparently, my sweatshirt.

"Probably a good idea," I said.

Her client looked up at me as if I was crazy.

I pressed back a smile and walked away wondering when I'd become the guy to tell a girl with an incredible body to cover up. Or, maybe I'd suggested it more out of self-preservation than out of worry for her discomfort. Or, maybe I was only having this stupid mind discussion because I was upset about Scotlyn.

I soaked the tubes in a bleach solution and then wiped them off before putting them in the ultrasonic cleaner. Stormy finished the leg tattoo and rang up her client. She joined me in the back room, no longer wearing the sweatshirt.

She looked pointedly down at her scantily clad body. "I

got the feeling you were a little put off by me borrowing the sweatshirt."

"No, I don't really mind. I'm just not in a great mood."

"Sorry to hear that." She turned up the radio as I slid the tubes into the sterilized bags to get them ready for the autoclave.

As I turned around, she slid past me, purposely making sure that her thigh brushed my hand. I leaned back against the counter and looked at her. She blinked up at me with innocent green eyes. "Look, Stormy, you are an amazing tattoo artist, and I'm really glad to have you in my shop—"

Her lip pushed out in a pout. "I know, Cassie told me you have a girlfriend." She smiled and ran her finger along the art on my arm. "I just thought, you know— for fun."

"As much as I love fun, and something tells me you would be a lot of fucking fun—" We were standing in the room where I'd drawn Scotlyn's tattoo to cover her long scar. With every inch of skin, and every soft sound from her otherwise mute lips, and every quickly scrawled note, I'd fallen harder and harder for Scotlyn. She was the only person I needed. I looked at Stormy. "Not going to happen."

Stormy shrugged. "That's cool. The offer remains on the table if you are ever up for it. I'll see you in the morning, boss."

Chapter 4

Scotlyn

Morning sun was poking around the curtains in the family room. I plucked up the empty beer cans and chip bag from the coffee table. I'd gotten home near midnight, and my head throbbed from memorizing glycolysis and the citric acid cycle. I knew Nix had been upset with me for blowing off his dinner plans, but I didn't want to miss a chance to study with the group. He had apparently filled himself on beer and chips and then gone off to bed.

I walked into the bedroom. He was still fast asleep. I stared down at him. He was just as handsome asleep as awake, and my heart always raced at the sight of him. I tiptoed around and collected up the clothes he'd dropped on the floor before climbing into bed. I yanked his wallet out of his pocket and set it on the nightstand. He turned over and stretched. The sheet slid off, exposing his naked, muscular back, and I badly wanted to slide back in bed with him. I glanced at the clock. I had a good half hour before I needed to dress for work. I decided I could make up for last night's disappointment, and satisfy my own needs, with a morning quickie.

I reached down and grabbed his sweatshirt and socks

and carried them to the clothes hamper. On the way, a cloud of perfume floated up from his sweatshirt. I pressed it to my face and took a deep breath. I rarely wore perfume, and this was definitely not mine. My stomach tightened as I stared down at the sweatshirt. Tears burned my eyes. I hadn't been acting myself around Nix, and deep down, I knew it was hurting him. The proposal had scared me. I wanted more than anything to marry Nix, but once I married him, he would be family and I'd lost family before. I couldn't go through it again. My silly, superstitious mind had convinced me that being part of my family was a dangerous thing. I'd never understood why I'd been spared from death that horrible day. And when the call from Diana came at the exact same moment as the proposal, my overactive imagination had at once settled in on it being a bad omen for marriage.

I heard the sheets rustle behind me. "Hey, baby, why don't you climb back in bed for awhile." His deep, drowsy voice rolled over my shoulder as I gazed at the perfume soaked sweatshirt.

I swallowed away the dryness in my throat. "I can't. I told Clutch I'd be in early to open for him. He is going to be late."

I heard the bed move as he turned back over.

I dropped the sweatshirt into the hamper and went in to shower off the horrid smelling perfume and the tears.

CHAPTER 5

Scotlyn

Nix's car was in the driveway, but the house was dark. Ten o'clock was early for him to be in bed. I didn't know if I was relieved or not. I wanted desperately to talk to him, but everything felt disconnected and cold right now. We seemed to have lost that one magical strand in our relationship that had always been perfect— our ability to communicate. Even when I could only speak through handwritten notes and gestures, Nix had known exactly what I was thinking as he listened with his eyes and his heart. We'd formed an instant attachment to each other, and for the first time, it felt as if that attachment had splintered.

I'd sat through a two hour lecture on phlebotomy and had hardly heard a word the professor said. My notes were scattered and disorganized, and now I would have to spend an hour rewriting them before next week's final.

I walked into the house, flicked on the light and laid my book bag on the kitchen chair. The house seemed extra quiet and dark. I tiptoed down the hall to our room to take off my shoes and change into something more comfortable for my note writing session. The bed was empty.

"Nix," I called toward the bathroom. No answer. Only

TESS OLIVER

his car was home.

I went back to the kitchen and pulled out my phone. No text. No message. It was not like him. And now, my overactive imagination would have fun trying to figure out where the heck he was. After finding the scented sweatshirt, I'd spent the drive to work and most of the morning trying to devise a story of how the perfume had gotten on Nix's sweatshirt. Clutch had said several things that went right past me, and he sensed that something was up. But, being Clutch, he didn't ask, and I was relieved. By my lunch break, I'd convinced myself that there was a reasonable explanation for the perfume and that I was just being silly. But coming home to an empty house and no message from Nix telling me why he'd be late had me fretting again. Of course, the logical thing to do would've been to call him, but I wasn't in the mood to be sensible.

My stomach ached with hunger. I grabbed a yogurt from the refrigerator and pulled out my notebook. The messy scribbles on the pages worried me. I only hoped I could make sense out of them. Most of my classmates used tape recorders during the lectures, but I found I learned more by writing notes during class. My years of silence had made me highly skilled with a pen, and my handwriting was nearly as speedy as my typing.

I stirred the strawberries around in my yogurt and took one bite. It tasted sour and unappealing. I dropped the spoon into the container. As empty as my stomach was, I had no appetite. My phone rang just as I picked up my pen, and my heart leapt a little. It was Taylor.

"Hey, Scottie, since the guys are out together, I figured it would be a good time to call. I need to ask you a favor."

"Wait, Taylor, did you say the guys were out together?"

She got quiet. "Why? Is Nix at home? Clutch told me they—" Her voice broke.

"No, Taylor, don't freak out. Nix isn't home. He must be with Clutch."

It took her a second to compose herself, and for a brief moment, I felt a little less ashamed about my own conclusion jumping.

"Shit, you scared me. I thought Clutch had lied to me. Nix didn't let you know they went out?"

I was embarrassed to have to admit it. "No, but I was in class, so he probably didn't want to bother me. But I'm sorry I scared you." I picked up the pen and doodled. "Shit, Taylor, do you ever wonder if these guys are worth the heartbreak? Sometimes, I envy that you don't live with Clutch. You still have some independence."

Her laugh spurted through the phone. "Independence? Have you met my mom and dad?"

I drew a heart with the word Nix in it and put down the pen. "I have, and you're right. What was I thinking? What was the favor?" I still had no explanation for Nix not telling me he was going out, but I felt better knowing where he was.

"My final project this quarter is to design a summer wedding dress."

I knew where this was going, and after the ill-timed proposal, being a model for a wedding dress was the last thing I wanted to do. "Taylor, can't you ask Cassie or Finley to model for you?"

"Oh, come on, Scottie, please? Finley and Cassie are

both too short to be good models."

"So, I get the honor because I'm an Amazon woman, is that what you're saying?"

"Let's face it— you look as if you stepped right out of a magazine. You're a perfect wedding dress model. Please. I even have your measurements from the business suit I designed last quarter. They are probably still the same. I can use those, and when the dress is nearly finished, we can do a fitting. You will hardly have to do a thing."

I sighed. "Fine. I'll do it."

"Yippee! I can't fail with a model like you. I could just cut arm holes in a pillowcase and attach a fluttery skirt and you'd be gorgeous."

"Thanks, Taylor. That's sweet of you."

There was a pause. "I've got to say, you sound a little down," Taylor said. "Everything all right?"

I swirled the spoon around in the yogurt. "Everything is great. I'm just tired, that's all. You know work and school— it's a lot."

"Yeah, I know what you mean."

"Where'd you say the guys went?"

"Not sure. Clutch said they were going out for burgers and beer. Hey, are you still going out to Finley's rescue barn on Saturday?"

The outing had seemed like so much fun, and I was dying to see the place, but at the moment, I had little enthusiasm for anything. Of course, sitting at home and moping around had even less appeal. Petting animals always made me happy. "Yep, I'm going."

"Great, see you then, and thanks for putting up with my design projects."

"Sure thing." I put my phone on the table and stared down at my notebook. Something told me my head wasn't on straight enough to decipher my notes tonight. I scooted the chair back and went in to wash up and get ready for bed.

From the bedroom, I could hear the loud stuttering motor of Clutch's Chevelle. The front door opened and shut. Nix's familiar footsteps sounded on the wood floor of the family room. Normally, just the sound of Nix walking into the house would make me smile, but I was feeling out of sorts and uneasy about everything. Nix and I hardly ever fought. There had been a few times when we'd been a little pissed about something, usually something that eventually gave us a good laugh and a reason for great make-up sex, but this time seemed different. The hardest thing about it was that whenever I was upset about something, or I'd had a bad day because my mind had fixated on my family's accident, or when things were just going shitty, Nix was my best friend. He was the one person who I needed to see or be held by to feel better. I couldn't turn to him, and I was feeling incredibly alone.

I finished washing my face and walked into the bedroom. Nix had turned on the stereo in the family room. I took a deep breath and walked out. His feet were propped up on the coffee table, and he stared at the blank television set with a beer can between his hands. Music rained down from the speakers overhead. From the heavy lidded look on his face, he was already drunk. He'd heard me walk into the room but didn't turn to look at me. And just that small, cold non-gesture felt like icy fingers taking hold of my heart.

"You went out with Clutch?"

He nodded and lifted the can to his mouth. I blinked back tears. Crying was the last thing I needed right now.

I walked into the kitchen and grabbed my notebook before heading back toward the hallway.

"Clutch wanted to go out because he'd been at work since six in the fucking morning and needed a break." His words were slowed by the alcohol. It was rare for him to get this drunk. I stopped and looked at him, confused about why he had the need to let me know about Clutch's work schedule. Especially since I worked with the man.

I was about to walk to the bedroom when the reason for him letting me know hit me. I'd used getting to work early to open up for Clutch as an excuse for not crawling back in bed with Nix. I stopped and stared down at the notebook in my hands. It had been stupid to include Clutch in my lie, but the unfamiliar perfume smell had knocked the wind from me. The getting to work early excuse was all I could come up with.

"Not sure what the hell is going on, Scotlyn, but you've never lied to me before."

His accusatory tone brought tears as I spun around to face him. His pale amber eyes were glazed and unfocused. He was drunker than I'd ever seen him.

"It seems trust is disintegrating on both sides of this relationship," I sobbed, and ran from the room. I would have given anything to have that superpower men seem to have to make women cry. Or, the ability to avoid crying when it was extremely counterproductive would have been nice too.

I heard his footsteps in the hallway behind me.

"Goddamnit, Scotlyn, talk to me. Tell me what the fuck is going on?" The hurt in his face was as agonizing as the ache in my chest. My throat seized up and the words lodged there. There were times when, if I was in enough despair, my voice would leave me again. I felt that strangling silence as I looked at him through my tears. I wanted to bring up the sweatshirt, but I was scared. I was afraid of his reaction. And so, I retreated to my safe haven of quiet.

It seemed he had to make a conscious effort not to sway on his feet. For the first time since we'd met, it felt as if we were two strangers staring at each other. I was torn between wanting to walk over and slap him and wanting to fall into his arms. As badly as I wanted this all to stop, it seemed, tonight, things had gotten a lot worse.

"So, now you're just going to stop talking? Great, why don't you just write it all down in your fucking notebook then." He turned and walked out. The sliding door opened and shut. The lounge scraped the cement floor of the patio.

I stood there in the center of the room so stunned by his words, I couldn't move.

CHAPTER 6

Nix

Sleeping on a lounge isn't so bad for an hour or two, especially if you're shitfaced, but an entire night on a chaise is a whole different thing. My head felt as if someone had driven nails through my skull with a drill. I hadn't gotten that drunk since I'd graduated high school and, with the way I was feeling, I wouldn't be doing it again anytime soon. Worst of all, I was going to suffer the agony of my stupidity all day at work and none of it had helped dull the pain I'd been feeling inside.

When Clutch had complained about having been at work since six in the morning, it'd felt as if someone had kicked me in the gut. I couldn't think of any reason why Scotlyn would have lied except that she didn't want to get in bed with me. And that was when I started ordering the shots. Clutch figured something was wrong, but he never pried. Although, after the sixth shot, he placed his big hand on my shoulder and said 'bro, whatever it is, that tequila is just going to make you hate life more in the morning'. Turns out, he'd been right.

The sun was still low in the summer sky, and it was surrounded by the infamous June gloom, the fuzzy mist that hung around in early morning. I was thankful for that cloud cover today. I sat up and looked around the small yard. Before Nana had died, we'd made the decision that Diana would take the cash assets, and I would get the house. Both were about equal in value, which made things easy.

Scotlyn and I loved this house. Scotlyn had planted flowers around the borders the way Nana had years before. Something about the wood fence, small expanse of yard and flowers had always reminded me of one of those vintage home pictures from the fifties where the mom would be standing dressed in her knee length dress and salon hairdo watching the boys play in perfectly clean striped t-shirts and greased down side parts.

The shower turned on. Scotlyn was getting ready for work.

My brain had been plastered last night, but I could still vividly recall the few minutes with Scotlyn. They were bad. Even in my hazy state of mind, her hurt expression had pressed into my memory, and I couldn't forget it. And somewhere during the tequila hurricane in my head, Scotlyn had mentioned something about our trust in each other disintegrating. I'd had no idea what she was talking about, and when she lapsed into frustrating silence, something she did whenever she was really upset or worried, I got pissed...and mean.

I got up and went into the kitchen to start coffee. It would take the whole damn pot to clear my muddy head today. There was a yogurt cup on the table with the spoon still in it. I picked it up to throw it away. She'd hardly touched it.

The shower turned off. There was no way we could both go to work today with this much shit between us. I walked into the bedroom just as Scotlyn came out of the bathroom with a towel on her head and dressed in only her bra and panties. She looked much thinner. As she reached up to pull the towel off, her rib cage looked far more prominent than I remembered. I'd been so self-absorbed in my own misery, I had apparently not noticed that she wasn't eating.

She seemed to sense what I was thinking and quickly reached for her shirt on the dresser. Her hands shook as she pulled it on.

I swallowed hard as she lifted her blue gaze to me. That same hurt was still there, and I wasn't completely sure how to wipe it away. "I'm sorry, baby, I was drunk. I'm stupid when I'm drunk. You know that."

She nodded.

"God, Scotlyn, please don't. We need to talk about this. I'm fucking dying here." As I spoke, tears streamed down her face, but I could sense that silence had gripped her. It was her mechanism for dealing with pain, but for me, it was pure frustration.

I stepped closer. Her face was just as beautiful in sorrow as in happiness. It was a face that I'd fallen in love with from just a crumpled up picture, and it still stole my breath every time I looked at her. She smelled of fresh soap, and citrus shampoo and everything that had been right in my life. I had to convince myself not to touch her. I wanted more than anything to pull her into my arms, but I dreaded her reaction. "Tell me what I've done, Scotlyn. Please don't shut me out. Please tell me why the hell this is coming apart? I've never needed anything as badly as I need you."

Her lips parted slightly, and for a second, it seemed that I'd broken down the wall. But then she reached for her jeans.

"Look, Scotlyn, we've got no house payment and things are going well at the shop. Why don't you ask Clutch if you can cut down on your hours? You'll have more time to spend on your homework. You're doing too much."

She sat down and pulled on her jeans.

I stared down at her. "Please, fucking talk to me, Scotlyn."

She peered up at me. Tears streamed down her pale cheeks. It seemed to take all her energy to speak. "I've never been on my own," she said weakly.

The ache in my head migrated to my chest. "Is that what you want?"

"Lincoln took care of me. Then you took care of me. But I've never been on my own."

My jaw clenched at the mention of his name. "So, you're comparing me to Lincoln?"

"No, that's not what I meant." Her body shook with sobs. "I like working and going to school and being a member of the world again. I wasn't part of it for a long time. Don't take that from me."

"Then what? What is it? Last night you mentioned something about trust. What have I done to make you mistrust me? You've got to give me something, baby. I'm going fucking nuts."

She shook her head, and the mute button was turned conveniently back on. She got up and went back into the bathroom, shutting the door behind her.

I walked out of the bedroom and had to convince myself not to throw my fist into a wall.

Chapter 7

Scotlyn

"You know, Cass, I think I'm going to skip today." I tucked the phone between my ear and shoulder and poured myself a cup of coffee. "I've got finals next week, and I should study."

"No, you've got to go. It'll be good for you. Warm, stinky barn animals staring up at you, begging for love and attention. Besides, Finley and Rett are really excited about us coming. Look, the sun is coming out early. It's going to be a beautiful day. And, I promise I won't even ask why Nix looks like shit. I won't bring up anything, unless you bring it up first. So put on your barn clothes. I'm picking you up in fifteen." Cassie was always good at the no arguments closing.

"All right. See you then."

I nibbled on the piece of toast that was more charcoal than bread. My appetite had shrunk severely, and I knew my weight was dropping. But I just couldn't work up the desire to eat. My heart was so broken, and my head was always in such a state of disarray, eating just took too much energy.

After I'd fallen into my usual, embarrassing blubbering state of tears and sobs, I'd lost my nerve to ask Nix about the sweatshirt. His harshness the night before, drunk or not, had been too much for me to bear. He'd never spoken to me so coldly, and I felt sick every time I thought about it. I hated always being so absurdly sensitive and easily upset. It was something that I still had not been able to conquer. Many people liked to shower me with praises of having courage and strength, but I couldn't see it. I was still a mess deep inside, and when things went awry, my courage and strength were easily toppled.

Nix had gone to work early, and I was glad to have the house to myself. I went to the bedroom and pulled out my jeans and boots. Finley had warned us not to wear sandals, unless we wanted toes smashed by hooves. My jeans suddenly seemed a size too large. Hopefully, a day outside at a barn would give me an appetite.

***

"Oh my gosh, this place is so darn cool." Taylor leaned forward to get a better view through the front windshield. "I love the red barns with the green trim." She sat back. "O.K., that's cuteness to the max. Do you guys see this?"

I unbuckled my seatbelt and scooted forward to get a view from the backseat. Rett was walking a mini horse out of one of the barns. He was wearing a white t-shirt, jeans and a cowboy hat.

"Shit, Rett dressed as Rett is already a fantasy, but Rett with a black cowboy hat pushed down low over that long blond hair—" Cassie said. "It's like having the world's hottest cowboy crash into the world's hottest surfer to make one incredibly outstanding man. If his picture cuddling little, rescued barn animals doesn't spur on donations then I have no right to use a camera." It was rare to hear Cassie gush on about any guy, but she was right— Rett made everything around him dim in comparison.

We watched him stroll toward us. A big, white smile broke out under the shade of his hat.

"Do you think he realizes the impact he has?" Cassie asked.

Taylor laughed. "Rett? Are you friggin' kidding? That boy worries when he doesn't turn every female head in a three mile radius."

"I never got the feeling that Rett thought much about his looks," I said.

"He doesn't think about his looks. He wakes up looking like that. But trust me, he knows about *impact*." Taylor opened the car door.

We all climbed out. The warm, pungent scent of hay, animals and manure drifted toward us. A cow standing in a nearby pen looked up from her pile of grass to check us out momentarily before lowering her big head down again. Cassie and I walked around to the trunk of the car, and I helped her with the equipment.

"Leave the tripod and flashes here, Scottie. I might not use them at all."

We each gave Rett a hug.

I stroked the small horse's neck.

Rett smiled down at his companion. "This is Zeus. He's twenty-eight years old. The owners were moving out of state to a condo. He thinks he's my dog, and if I don't take him along on rounds, he starts to whiny like a mad man."

Cassie was already snapping pictures. She had this innate talent for capturing emotion and the spirit of the moment. Her portfolio was filled with pictures that read like a book. Once, without them knowing, she'd snapped a picture of Nix sitting at Nana's bedside. The two of them were laughing about something Nana had said. Cassie had sent it to me in an email, and the second I opened it, tears filled my eyes. You could see their love for each other almost as if was a visible, solid entity floating in the air between them. I printed the picture and had it framed.

Taylor rubbed the horse's ears. "You have become quite the animal lover, haven't you, Rett? I know you guys weren't raised with many pets, so it's cool to see how easily you've learned all this."

"You didn't think I had it in me, huh, Tater Tot?" He flicked the brim of his hat up out of his line of vision.

Cassie raised her camera. "Ooh, push your hat down and do that again. You looked like Redford as Sundance Kid."

"Yeah?" Rett seemed pleased with the comparison. He obliged, and Cassie took the picture.

Finley was pulling off gloves as she came out of the barn. Just as Rett had looked like some incredible cowboy surfer hybrid, Finley, with her white blonde rock and roll hair cut, piercings and work boots, looked like a rock star farmer hybrid. Together, they were stunning and adorable. They looked incredibly happy, which made me suddenly miss Nix terribly.

Cassie shot a picture of Finley as she tucked her gloves in her back pocket. "You are just in time. Yesterday, we got three baby goats from a breeder who had too many goats to take care of properly. Three does that are being bottle fed."

"We get to bottle feed baby goats?" Taylor asked excitedly.

"If you're up for it?" Finley smiled my way.

"Absolutely," I answered. "It'll probably be the best thing I've done all month."

Cassie peeked in my direction, but she'd been keeping to her promise about not asking me anything. And I was glad. For now, I was ready to forget my problems and get lost in the world of wet noses and plush ears. We followed Finley to the barn.

"Fin, I'm going to put Zeus in the pasture and start mucking pens," Rett said.

"Thanks, sweetie."

Cassie stopped and shot a picture of him walking away with his little horse. It was going to be a cute damn picture, one that I never would have had the forethought to take, which was why Cassie was the photographer.

Finley had this amazingly graceful and speedy walk that was almost hard to keep up with. The three of us hurried behind. Several chickens scurried past us as we stepped into the dank shade of the barn. A flurry of tiny squeaking noises came from behind a stall door. I glanced over it. Three baby goats stared up at me, bleating like three hungry babies.

"Oh my gosh, they are absolutely the cutest things ever." I looked over at Finley. "How old are they?"

"Three weeks. They'll need the bottle until they are about eight weeks, but they are starting to nibble on hay."

Finley disappeared into a small room. A few minutes later, she stepped back out with three baby bottles of milk. She tested a drop from each one on her forearm. This was a girl who'd suffered from debilitating anxiety that prevented her from leaving the house, and now she'd overcome it to help animals live a quality life. She had told me about losing her sister to a flu virus that Finley had brought home from school. For years, Finley had believed that she was the cause of her sister's death. While I'd never blamed myself for our car accident, I had lived with some horrible guilt. I'd wanted to sit in the front seat, and I'd lied to my mom, telling her the backseat made me carsick on mountain roads. She'd given me her seat and I had survived. It was a lie that would haunt me for the rest of my life. Finley had dealt with her loss and guilt by sealing herself away from the world. I'd sealed myself away too, in a silent world.

"Taylor, grab that milking stool over there." Finley motioned to a stool with short legs sitting outside the stall. "There's one inside already. The goats love to jump on things."

We slid into the stall. It was filled with straw and a smell that I assumed was distinctively *goat.* The tiny does stood up on back hooves, pressing their tiny front hooves against Finley's legs. The ruckus they made was so comical, it was impossible not to laugh.

"These are African Pygmy goats. Baby goats are called kids." Finley explained. She handed me a bottle and pointed to one of the stools. "Just hold it out, and they'll latch on. You'll be amazed how fast they can drain these bottles."

Cassie was checking out the light in her lens. "I'm going to take pictures while you feed them. Not completely sure how they'll turn out, but I hate to miss this."

Finley gave a bottle to Taylor, and she shared my stool. A tiny caramel colored muzzle grabbed onto the rubber nipple. "Yep, I was right," I said. "Best thing I've done all month. Maybe all year."

Finley glanced over my shoulder. "That's Trixie. She's sort of the queen bee right now. They're herd animals. They don't like to live without other goats, but there is always a pecking order. Later, we can put them out in a pen and watch them play. They are so cute together. They get really rowdy, head butting each other and jumping up on their little slide."

"They have a slide?" Taylor asked.

"They love it. But most of the time they just jump from the top."

"Well, yeah, who doesn't?" Taylor looked around for corroboration. "Oh, come on, none of you jumped from the top of the slide when the yard supervisor wasn't looking?"

Cassie was clicking away. "My school only had old rubber tires set up like an army training camp," she said from behind her lens. "These are such great pictures." She lowered the camera. "I really think I can get a nice set of photos that will get the word out about this place. Jade, the reporter who came out here yesterday, wrote a really great article. She let me read it to give me an idea of what kind of shots to get."

"Does Some Pig hang out here with you?" Taylor asked. "And what was your cow's name?"

"Lilly Belle. Some Pig no longer identifies with the pig world. As far as he's concerned, he is a short, stout human who just happens to walk on all four feet. My fault, I'm afraid. But I think it would scar him mentally to let him know he's a pig. And, as for Lilly Belle, I think she'd protest too. She has her own little pasture and barn on my dad's estate. No pesky neighbors to steal her hay."

The bottles were sucked dry. One of the goats jumped into Finley's lap. "Sorry, Emmie, the bottle is dry. You'll have to wait a few hours for the next one. They're eating about every four hours right now."

"I want to get some outside shots," Cassie said. "And the three of us were noting how great Rett looked in his cowboy hat."

Finley got up and we followed her out. "It's awesome, right? I picked it out for him and was not disappointed in my choice."

We said goodbye to the goats and followed Finley out to some semi-covered pens. "All three of these horses came from the race track. If they have lameness issues or other problems that keep them from racing, they are discarded as useless. We took them in before they were auctioned off for slaughter. Two can be rehabilitated, and eventually, we'll find a nice horse lover to adopt them."

Rett came around the corner. "Hey, sweetie," Finley called to him, "we need big money to keep this place going. So take off that t-shirt and get over here with that mucking fork and those shoulder muscles. Cassie's going to take some pictures."

Rett put on a good show of acting shocked. We all watched with great interest as he rested the fork against the fence and took off his hat. He reached back and pulled off his shirt. We gave him a nice round of applause and wolf calls.

"I'm feeling pretty damn cheap and used right now," Rett said.

"And you love it," Taylor quipped.

"Hell yes, I do." He picked up the fork and pressed on his hat. His long blond hair turned up on his bare shoulders.

Cassie waved her hand to show him where the light was best. "Just be Rett. You don't have to pose. Just do your thing, and this place will be swimming in donations."

"I could drop the jeans too. Just boots and a hat," Rett suggested.

Finley glanced over at us. "And he would too." She turned back to him. "That's very generous of you, sweetie, but we need to leave something to the imagination."

CHAPTER 8

Scotlyn

By noon, the sun was bearing down on the ranch. I'd fed chickens, been chased by two geese, helped corral four sheep back into their pasture and helped hose down the pig pens. Cassie had been right. Hanging out with animals, wonderful creatures who were finally in situations where they could feel safe and comfortable, had been good for me.

Finley and Taylor went in to make lunch while I played with the goats in their yard. Cassie waited patiently behind her camera and clicked off dozens of shots. I sat on the end of the slide, and all three kids hopped into my lap at once. I laughed and squeezed them all against me.

"Got it," Cassie said. Then she lifted her phone and took another shot. She looked at it and pressed some stuff on her phone. "I had to send that one to Nix."

"Cassie," I said. "You didn't?"

"I did. It's so cute. He's been so grumpy. It'll cheer him up." She lowered her camera. "You're not mad, are you?"

I shook my head. "No, I'm not."

She sat on the fence. "I know I promised not to ask, but

is there anything you want to talk about? Nix is in a really bad way. I've never seen him like this." She chuckled. "Yesterday, he put the wrong stencil on this big old biker dude's leg. It was the butterfly for the next client, an eighteen year old girl who was getting a tattoo for her birthday. Thank goodness he noticed before he started inking it in."

"God, that could have been disastrous." The goats took turns jumping on and off of my lap. They reminded me of cartoon characters, springing off all four legs at once. "Nix proposed to me," I blurted.

Cassie nodded. "He said the call about Nana came in right as he showed you the ring."

"It definitely cast a shadow on what was supposed to be an exciting moment in my life."

She placed a hand on my arm. "Coincidences happen. You can't read anything into it." Cassie knew I had a silly tendency to be superstitious.

"I know this is ridiculous, but I feel that if we get married then Nix will officially be part of my family and—"

"—and you've lost your family before." A goat hopped into her lap, and she rubbed its back. "Scottie, everything in life is a risk. Just giving our hearts to these guys is a huge risk." She laughed. "I mean, look what happened to me. I would be working at a magazine in New York still if Dray hadn't been here silently begging me to come back by doing what he does best, getting into trouble."

"You do keep him grounded, and he adores you, Cass." I put my arm around her shoulder. "And with good reason."

"Thanks. And, if ever there was someone who needed grounding, it's Dray." She was quiet for a second, and it was obvious she was thinking about him. She'd had a huge crush on him long before Dray had finally come to his senses and realized they were meant to be together. She looked over at me. "I feel like you're not telling me everything."

I sighed. "The proposal, losing Nana and my fear of losing Nix has made me sort of pull away from him. Without meaning to, I've fallen back into that same solitary world I constructed after I lost everyone I cared about. I've been kind of distant and just at a time when Nix probably needed me the most." I swallowed hard and wondered if I would sound silly and paranoid for bringing up the sweatshirt. But besides me, Cassie knew Nix better than anyone. "The other morning, I was picking up Nix's clothes off the floor, as usual—"

She laughed. "It's like they were raised in—" She glanced around. "Well, in a barn."

I chuckled. "I picked up his sweatshirt, and it had a really strong smell of perfume on it. Not my perfume. In fact, I hardly ever wear the stuff."

Cassie seemed to be contemplating what I said. "Perfume? That doesn't make sense, Scottie. Nix is over the top crazy about you. He would never cheat on you."

"I know, but I've been so cold to him, I can't help wondering if I pushed him into some other girl's arms."

"Perfume," she repeated. "Wait a minute. The new tattoo artist, Stormy—" She rolled her eyes as she said the name. "You haven't met her yet, have you?"

I shook my head but wasn't thrilled with the way this was going. "Nix said she's really talented, but I know nothing about her."

65

"The girl bathes in perfume. It's a sort of spicy, not super expensive smelling concoction, sort of like her. They smacked into each other as she was coming around the corner. The perfume probably transferred to his clothes. I'm not kidding, the shop is under a cloud of it all day. Yesterday, Nix finally told her to stop wearing so much. I couldn't stop sneezing."

"Then I feel really foolish." I pressed my hand against my forehead. "And then I made up a lie about going to work early. Shit, I've really messed things up. Poor Nix." Relief washed through me, but I wanted to kick myself for being such a paranoid ninny. I would have to make it up to him. And I'd have to find the courage to tell him why I'd been so distant. "Surely, he's convinced that I've been acting strangely because I don't want to marry him. I don't know when I'll ever be able to shake off what's happened to me. I want so badly just to be happy, but I'm always worried about losing people I love. I think Nana's death just triggered those deep seated fears again."

"Look, Scottie, you'll never shake what happened. It was something so enormous, you'll never be able to outpace it. But we all fear losing the people we love. I can't even imagine how much greater that fear grows once you have a baby. Losing people is all part of life. What you suffered is far worse than most people will ever have to endure, but you're strong. And now you're becoming a nurse, which is so damn great. I know Nix is really proud of you."

My eyes ached with tears. I hugged Cassie. "Thanks. I think Nix and I will have to have a long talk tonight. I owe him an apology."

"I think he's going to Tank's Gym tonight to watch the

fights. But maybe he won't be too late."

"See, I didn't know that." My shoulders drooped again. "We're barely talking anymore. But I will make it right tonight. I have to. This is getting too hard."

A cowbell clanged. "Lunch," Finley called from the small trailer at the front of the property.

Cassie laughed. "A cowbell for calling us in for lunch. I love it. And just in time." She looked pointedly at me. "It looks like you're shrinking away to a skeleton."

"Some girls eat gallons of ice cream when they're upset or heartbroken. I can't get any food past my lips without wanting to gag on it."

"Shit, last time Dray and I had a fight, I baked an entire tray of brownies and by the end of the day, only the slightly burned edges were left." She tapped her chin. "Can't remember what it was, but Mr. Hothead stomped out of the house muttering his usual string of cuss words. It was something stupid, no doubt, but I'm used to it. After Dray cools off, he usually stomps right back in and snatches me from whatever I'm doing to make it up to me with sex. So, an occasional spat can be worth it." We left the pen, and the goats returned to their antics on the slide. "Talk to Nix tonight, have some wild sex and everything will be better in the morning."

Chapter 9

Nix

"That is the third time you've looked at that picture since we got here," Clutch's deep voice rolled down over my shoulder.

I flicked off the phone and stuck it in my pocket. One really annoying thing about having a friend as tall as Frankenstein was his ability to look over my shoulder. "And what the hell is your point?"

He laughed. "Hell, Nix, if you can't figure out my point then you've been inhaling too many ink fumes."

"It's a great picture. Cassie has tons of talent."

"Yeah, you're staring at a picture of Scottie because Cassie has so much talent."

I looked up at him. "Shut up."

"Yep."

People were still pouring into Tank's Gym. The crush of bodies and smell of sweat, cheap after-shave and whatever other gross odors a room full of men could produce made me rethink my decision to take Dray up on his invite. "Hey, nosy friend, put on your human periscope hat and check the room for Dray. I haven't seen him since we squeezed into

TESS OLIVER

this sardine can."

Clutch looked around. "Don't see him, but he's hard to spot in a crowd like this unless he's in the middle of a brawl. And since he's running the joint now, those spontaneous fights seem to have taken a backseat to his managerial position. Got to say, I kind of miss those knuckle bruisers." He glanced over at me. "Fuck, we're turning into those guys."

"Who are *those* guys?"

"Those guys who sip fucking vodka on the rocks and who take their women to reservation-only restaurants and who don't get into any good bar fights. I sure hope they make dress slacks in size thirty-eight long."

I lifted a brow at him. "Dress slacks?"

"Yep, can't sip vodka unless you're wearing fucking dress slacks."

I laughed. "The day you wear a pair of slacks, and Dray stops throwing his fist at the slightest provocation, is the day I turn Freefall into a tea shop."

"There's Rett," Clutch said. "And it looks like Dray is following him over here."

I scooted forward and away from the dude who was talking super loud to his friend about a threesome he was in the night before. His friend didn't look too inclined to believe him. I was tired of listening to him and having his stale breath cross my face every two seconds. "Don't know why the hell I thought this would be a good place to hang tonight." My mood had shifted from feeling completely lost and heartbroken to completely pissed and frustrated, and I had no idea which way to look next. My work day had been busy, but it had been hard keeping my mind on the tattoos.

When Cassie, my extremely devious and highly skilled photographer friend, had sent over the incredible picture of Scotyln laughing and cuddling baby goats, I couldn't stop looking at it. That bittersweet feeling of knowing there was no one in the world for me but her, and at the same time not understanding what was happening between us, threw off my concentration for the rest of the day.

"Hey, glad you guys came," Dray said. "Place is fucking packed."

"Yeah, what the hell?" I asked. "You better hope the fire marshal doesn't make a surprise visit."

"Thanks, for that," Dray said. "Like I'm not already fucking stressed enough. These fights were supposed to take place across town, so the place is crawling with douchebags who aren't locals. And some of them look less than reputable. Just hope I don't have to put on my bouncer uniform tonight."

The loudspeaker crackled on overhead. "Dray, we need you at the ticket booth."

"Shit," he muttered. "We're about to start. See you later." Dray pushed back through the crowd.

Rett was wearing a blue bandana around his neck that his brother zeroed in on instantly. "Hey, Billy the Kid, finished rustling cattle already?"

"As a matter of fact, yeah. You got a problem with my attire?"

Clutch shook his big head. "Nope. Really, Barrett, good job. I'm glad you found something you like to do."

Rett held back a grin. Recognition from his older brother was like gold to the guy.

We pushed closer to the octagon, but with the press of bodies behind us and the bobbing heads and stretching necks in front of us, it was going to be tough to get a good view of the fight. Clutch usually came in handy for carving a clear path, but even he wasn't having any luck tonight.

The side doors opened, and we waited for the first pair of fighters to emerge when Dray's voice came through the loudspeaker. "Would the giant with the oversized head please duck down? No one can see over you." Dray was up on the catwalk over the office that Tank had built to keep an eye on the place during occasions like this. He was holding the microphone as he smiled down at us through the clutter of heads.

Attention around us spun to Clutch. Clutch's big arm lifted in the air, and he lifted his middle finger to Dray.

"Would the giant with the big head like to come up here and show me that gesture again?" Dray asked.

"Yes, the giant would," Clutch yelled back. The exchange was entertaining an otherwise restless crowd, who were now hot, sweaty and anxious for some action. The locals knew that this was just a joke between friends, but the out-of-towners seemed to think an awesome brawl was about to explode between the manager and the oversized spectator.

Clutch shook his head at me. "He sits up there sweet and pretty on his cute, little catwalk while we're stuck in this festering pool of stink. And if he doesn't get those fights started soon, shit is going to fly in here."

"Hey, giant, get your ass up here, and bring those two pretty boys with you. Especially the blond with the bandana." More laughter. Dray motioned for us to walk over.

He lifted the microphone to his mouth. "Unless you prefer to stand down there," he said in a tone that seemed to be just for our ears, but a room filled with people could hear it. Amused looks turned angry as we made our way through the crowd to the best seats in the house.

Rett smiled back at me. "I guess it pays to know people in high places."

"Literally."

We reached the rickety ladder that led to the platform where Dray sat on a metal chair. He'd pulled a second chair and bench up there. "These are the expensive ticket seats," he said. "Hopefully this rusted sheet of metal will hold all of us, otherwise we could end up flattening an entire row of people underneath."

He yanked out a small ice chest. "Even brought some refreshments." He pulled out beers and tossed one to each of us.

"I feel like a goddamn VIP at the Super Bowl," I said. "This is better. Thanks, man."

"I take care of my own," Dray said. We lifted our cans and tapped them together. "Let's drink one for Nana."

"For Nana," I said, and Clutch and Rett followed.

***

The evening had been going smoothly, but Dray had been keeping his eye on a sketchy looking group who'd come from across town. Their guys kept losing, and a cloud of tension was rising over them like a cloud of hot stink. Each one was carrying a flask, and they were taking as many swigs as their fighters were taking hits. Two of them had shaved heads that were covered in some pretty shabby looking ink. Their two buddies both looked like the kind of assholes who would eat kittens for lunch.

Dray leaned forward and rested his arms on his thighs. His hands were tight in fists, which was never a good sign. "I'm fucking glad to be getting out of here for a few days."

"Are you going with Cassie up to Yosemite for that photo shoot this week?" I asked.

"Yep, she talked me into it. Tank said he had the week free. I need a break from this place. And something tells me, after tonight, I'll really need it."

As the pair of fighters entered the ring, the four assholes elbowed their ways through the spectators to get a better view. Angry looks and cussing followed them, but most people got out of their way.

"I know they walked in with this fighter. Hope he has some skills," Dray said. "Otherwise, this ain't going to be pretty. Last time I guest host for another club. We've got some regulars here at Tank's, who sometimes need their asses straightened out, but it never goes further than that."

Rett looked over at him. "That's because they know the manager."

Dray nodded. "True. My reputation as being a bit explosive does help."

"A bit explosive?" Clutch repeated. "Shit, if you were Mount Vesuvius this place would be buried under layers of ash already."

Rett and I laughed. My phone buzzed in my pocket, and I pulled it out. It was a text from Scotlyn. Just seeing her name sent a rush of adrenaline through me.

"What time will you be home?"

"Not sure." I typed back.

"I think we need to talk."

"Yeah." I had no idea if her suggestion to talk was good or bad. I'd always known what Scotlyn was thinking or how she was feeling, but I'd lost that thread. I had no idea what was going on in her mind, and it was fucking with my head plenty.

"I guess I'll see you later," she wrote back.

"All right." I returned the phone to my pocket.

Clutch looked over at me. "Everything all right?"

"Wish I fucking knew." There was no way I was going to be able to pay attention to anything now. I leaned forward and looked over at Dray. "You know, I think I'm going to head home. Things haven't been too smooth this week, and I need to see what's going on."

Dray looked at Clutch. "Do you fucking believe this? The Heartbreak Kid—" He pointed at me and then at Rett. "And his heir to the heartbreak throne. One is running home to the girl to see how he can beg his way back into her panties, and the other is wearing a fancy neckerchief just to make his lady happy." Sometimes Dray didn't know when to shut up, but he was always good at sensing when he'd crossed the line. He noticed my face. "Look, bro, I'm just kidding. This is a lousy bunch of fighting marshmallows tonight anyhow. Go home and make nice with Scottie." He looked at Rett. "You and your fancy bandana— I've got nothing to say."

Rett shrugged. "That's because you are fucking clue-

75

less." He reached up to the bandana and gave it a tug. "If you knew some of the things I've done with this handy square of cloth, then you'd be shutting your big trap and begging me for ideas."

Dray's eyes went wide. "What? You tying her up?"

Rett didn't answer, but a smug grin crossed his face.

Dray got down on a knee and bowed low. "My lord, you have not disappointed me after all, and later, I want to be filled in on techniques."

Clutch rolled his eyes my direction. "What do you want to bet the next time we see Dray, he's got one of those damn bandanas around his neck?"

I looked at Dray. His eyes were gleaming. It seemed Rett had set his dirty mind into full motion. An angry shout from below carried our attention back to the floor.

Dray and Rett stood. A grunt of sympathy rolled through the crowd. "Shit, their fighter is out. I better get down there."

Clutch looked up at him. "Do you want us to come along?"

The people below seemed to vibrate with agitation suddenly, and the first shove match had begun. "What do you think?" Dray asked.

We got up and followed him down to the floor. I looked back at Clutch. "Don't bother looking for those extra long slacks. We aren't *those* guys, yet."

Dray shook his head as we reached the edge of onlookers. "It's like those unwanted relatives at Thanksgiving. You work hard to plan a nice, cozy event, and they come in and fuck things up." He looked at us. "If we get those four out, then I think things will calm down." He whistled to a couple of Tank's regulars, big dudes with knuckles that nearly dragged the cement floor. They lumbered over with hungry looks in their eyes. Dray took a deep breath. "Let's go." He plunged through the flurry of fists and elbows and we followed.

CHAPTER 10

Scotlyn

After a long day at the barn, we were beat. Cassie and I stopped off to eat on the way home. The active day in the fresh air and the talk with Cassie had helped restore some of my appetite.

I'd showered, pulled on a long t-shirt, that I had basically stolen from Nix, and dropped onto the couch with my class notes. Nix hadn't been super enthusiastic in the few texts he'd sent back, but I knew he was in the middle of watching fights. I was anxious for him to get home, and even though I tried to concentrate on studying, I seemed to be reading the same lines over and over again, and everything was bouncing off my muddled brain. I stretched out on the couch, and with a full stomach for the first time in weeks, I drifted off into a deep sleep.

An hour later, the front door lock clicked open. I sat up and rubbed my eyes. I placed my books and notes on the coffee table and stood from the couch just as Nix stepped inside the house.

"Your face," I gasped. There was a cut running parallel with his eyebrow and his bottom lip was swollen. He didn't say a word but watched me through long lashes as I assessed the damage. "What happened?"

"Nothing. Dray just needed help bouncing a few guys from Tank's. I met a flying, ring-covered fist somewhere in the confusion."

"Sit on the couch, and I'll get the first aid box and some ice." I turned to leave, but he took hold of my arm. Slowly, I faced him, and immediately, traitorous tears filled my eyes.

"Scotlyn, what's going on?"

I bit my bottom lip. He shook his head. "Don't you dare suck in that bottom lip, baby. Talk to me."

I took a breath. "Let me at least get something to clean that cut and then I'll talk. I promise."

I hurried into the bathroom and reached beneath the cupboard for the kit I'd put together for occasions like this. It seemed they happened often whenever Dray was involved. My hands shook as I took out the antibacterial ointment, sterile gauze and bandages.

Nix was sitting on the couch when I returned. The anguish in his face did nothing to bolster my courage. I knew he wanted to understand why I hadn't brought up the proposal again, but I would start with the easier, silly subject of me acting like a jealous fool.

I put the supplies on the table and knelt next to him. He turned to face me, and almost instantly, his hands went around my bare thighs. His chest rose and fell with deep breaths as his palms smoothed over my legs.

I put some ointment on the gauze. He winced as I wiped it over the cut. "It's almost deep enough to need stitches."

"No stitches." His hands trailed up to my panties, and a low groan rolled up from his chest. "Shit, it has been so fucking long since I've touched you, I'm aching all over from it."

I swallowed hard. "I'm sorry I lied to you the other morning. Believe it or not, I was planning to climb into bed with you before you'd even suggested it." I reached for some more gauze.

"What stopped you?"

I smiled. "It's something really stupid, and I'm embarrassed about it now."

While he waited for my explanation, he dragged my panties down and caressed my naked bottom. I sucked in a breath and closed my eyes as he leaned forward and kissed my neck. "This makes first aid a little tough."

"Your story," he said, as his mouth moved along my neck.

"I picked up your sweatshirt. It smelled strongly of a girl's perfume."

He pulled his mouth away and peered up at me.

"It's all right. Cassie told me the new girl at the shop wears a lot of perfume and that she ran into you as she came around the corner."

He lowered his hands. His expression hardened. "You thought I cheated on you?"

I tried to laugh it away. I lifted the bandage to his face, but he blocked it with his hand. "Scotlyn, did you seriously believe that I would cheat on you?"

The words were getting stuck again, and his harsh expression wasn't helping. I swallowed the dryness in my throat. I had to stop shrinking into silence every time things got rough. It frustrated Nix, but it was even more aggravat-

TESS OLIVER

ing for me.

I met his hurt gaze with mine. I took a deep breath. "I don't know, Nix. What would you do if you picked up my shirt and it smelled of another man's aftershave?"

"I'd go out and fucking kill the man who touched you." He shoved the coffee table away with his foot. He had obviously just come from a testosterone, adrenaline pumped evening, and all of it was still coursing through his veins. He walked to the center of the room and raked his fingers through his hair as if he was deciding what to punch. He turned back to me, and the look on his face made me sit back hard on the couch. "But I wouldn't be pissed at you, Scotlyn, because I would never think that you cheated on me."

I blinked back tears and stood up. "That's because you're so fucking confident, Mr. Heartbreaker, that you think no girl would dare cheat on the always loved and admired Nix Pierce." I hadn't meant any of it, of course, but I'd found the courage to fight back, and now stupidity flowed to widen the river bed between us. "I don't have that much confidence. After everything that's happened to me, I'm always expecting the worst. I figure what's another layer of heartbreak when I've already endured everything shitty life has to offer."

He pointed at me. "You don't get to do that. You don't get to pull out your ammo of 'life has been bad to me' to cover for the fact that you don't trust me. I've never done anything but love you, Scotlyn. I've never given you one fucking shred of reason not to trust me."

Earlier in the evening, I'd practically laughed this off, and I'd been sure he would too. I'd always known Nix so well. How could I not have seen that this would hurt him. "I'm sorry, Nix. I don't know how to take it all back." And that was it. My throat filled with sand like it always did when silence sucked in around me. I couldn't utter another word. I ran into the bedroom and shut the door behind me. I slid down against the wall and wrapped my arms around my knees and brought them to my chest. At least the unhelpful rivers of tears had stopped. I just didn't have any more to shed. I thought this was going to be the night that Nix and I started to mend what we had, but I seemed to have only succeeded in ripping us further apart.

CHAPTER 11

Nix

I peeled myself off the couch. The fight the night before had left me with cuts and bruises, but the argument with Scotlyn had hurt way more. I'd heard her leave the house, but I didn't get up to talk to her. I was still sorting shit out, trying to decide if I was the one being the asshole or if I truly had a reason to be pissed. I could only assume she'd gone to the coffee shop to meet her study group. There was a text from Clutch to call him and a voicemail from Stormy.

"Hey, Stormy, what's up?"

"Hey, world's sexiest boss, would you mind if I did a tattoo today? I know the shop is usually closed on Sunday, but this friend of mine works all week and Saturday. It should only take a few hours."

"No, that's fine. I've got some paperwork to do anyhow. I'll meet you at the shop in an hour."

"Great. See you then."

Clutch called the second I hung up. "Hey, what's up?"

"How's that cut on your eye?"

"Still there."

"That's why it helps to have a face that is too high up for anyone to reach with a fist. Anyhow, I think I found the beach rental. It'll fit all of us, and it's right on the sand."

I leaned back against the couch. "Yeah, I don't know if Scotlyn and I are going to go. Things are pretty unstable right now."

"Oh, come on. You've got to go. It's a tradition. You two will patch things up. For fucksake, you're Nix and Scotlyn, the dream couple."

"Yeah, dreams fade when you wake up, you know?"

"This one doesn't. Let's head down to the coast. I'm taking the Corvette and putting down the top. We can check out the house and get some lunch at that burger hut on the pier."

"Sounds romantic."

"Damn right it is. I'll pick you up in an hour."

"All right, but make it an hour and a half and pick me up at Freefall. I'm going to go open up the shop for Stormy."

"Stormy?"

"My new artist. I told you about her, but you always have your head in the clouds...metaphorically and literally. See you in ninety."

***

I had paperwork to do, but my mind was definitely not in it. Clutch walked in behind Stormy. She pursed her lips and pointed up at him.

"I've seen you at some of the local vintage car meets.

You are hard to miss."

Clutch seemed pleased with that assessment.

"Stormy, this is Jimmy, or Clutch as most people call him."

"Right, Clutch. You restore cars." She looked over at me. "Come to think of it, I've seen you at the meets too. I don't know why it took me so long to remember."

Clutch grinned down at her. "Nix is far less memorable."

She smiled and moved closer to me. Her hand rested on my arm. "I wouldn't say that at all."

I pulled my arm out from under her hand. "We're going to head out, so just remember to set the alarm before you leave."

She tucked her hands in the back pockets of her short shorts and made a point of pushing her cleavage out for view. Clutch nearly toppled forward like a felled tree in his attempt to get a closer look.

Stormy was pleased with the attention. "Got it. I won't forget. See you both later."

Clutch followed me out, and the door shut behind us. "That chick wants you."

"I think the boob flash was for both our benefits, and don't let it go to your head. Stormy seems to thrive on having all the attention in the room focused on her. She's a damn good tattoo artist though.

Clutch climbed into the car. He'd adjusted the seat so that it would accommodate his long legs, something he'd had to do with every car, but the Corvette was just too damn small for him. If it hadn't been convertible his head would've been pressed against the ceiling. "She's pretty damn hot, but she wears too much perfume."

"Yeah, and that's toned down. I had to tell her it was too much. Poor Cassie kept sneezing. And that perfume got me in some heavy fucking trouble. The air conditioner was blasting in that back room and Stormy pulled on my sweatshirt."

Clutch pulled away from the curb. "Shit, she's wearing your stuff? Then she really wants you."

I ignored his comment. "Anyhow, Scotlyn picked up the sweatshirt and—"

We stopped at a light. Clutch's booming laugh frightened the driver next to us. "So, Scottie smelled perfume and thought you were banging the new tattoo artist. Classic."

"I'm glad you think it's classic. I was fucking pissed that she would think that. I've never had eyes for anyone but her since we met. Thought she knew that, but I was wrong."

The sun was beating down on us as Clutch turned onto the freeway. "Are you fucking kidding me? What else would she think? Taylor would have nailed my ass to the wall if she'd smelled perfume on my clothes."

I stared out at the scenery that blurred past us as Clutch shifted into fifth. The car motor quieted as he reached a level speed. "Crap, maybe I overreacted. I was really fucking hurt thinking that she didn't trust me."

"What the hell, Saint Nix? You must put yourself on a pretty high fucking pedestal then to think you're above suspicion."

"I don't know what I was thinking. Everything just keeps

getting twisted up, and we can't seem to find our way out of the knots. You're right. I'm a total idiot." The freeway was crowded for a Sunday, and a trip to the beach seemed long and hot now. But Scotlyn wouldn't be home for hours, and I needed to think of what I was going to say to erase my stupidity. "Where's Taylor today?"

"She's working on that wedding dress for Scottie."

My face snapped toward him. "What?"

"It's some final project. She has to design a summer wedding dress, and Scottie is the model."

I nodded. "That is fucking ironic," I said quietly.

"Huh?"

"Oh, nothing." My phone buzzed. It was a text from Scotlyn.

"I'm going to stay at Cassie's for a few days to take care of her canaries while they're up north."

I stared at the text. There was no way canaries needed a full-time sitter. "You're not coming home at all?" Just typing the words made my stomach turn.

"I think this will be good," she wrote. "For the both of us."

I didn't respond, but I wanted to throw my phone out of the damn car. Clutch sensed my mood change.

"Uh oh. Looks like things just took a bad turn," he said.

"Holy shit, Clutch. What the fuck have I done?"

CHAPTER 12

Scotlyn

The orange canaries sang to themselves as I finished my coffee. Cassie's walls were covered with her pictures, each one a perfect snapshot of a moment in time. Every emotion showed through as if I was standing in the photo with the subject, experiencing everything along with them. Of course, Nix and I were in many of the pictures, and as hard as it was to look at them, it was even harder to look away. In one picture, Nix had picked me up to carry me over a puddle. I was laughing hysterically. I could still remember the moment as if it had just happened. Aside from a glorious early childhood with two loving parents, I have never been happier than I've been with Nix.

Cassie had asked if I would check in on the birds while they were away. But after the gut-wrenching night with Nix, I'd asked her if I could stay at her place until they returned. She, of course, told me I could stay as long as I liked. She didn't ask why, but her worry was evident in her tone.

I'd started this short separation, hoping it would give both of us a chance to straighten out our thoughts. But all it had done for me was make me nearly sick with missing

Nix. I had no idea what he was feeling or thinking. He'd been so upset with me for not trusting him, I didn't know if he'd ever forgive me. One thing was certain, it would change our relationship forever.

I couldn't eat or sleep or think. After working my butt off all quarter to excel in my classes, I'd more than likely screwed up my entire grade point average by fumbling my way through the finals. I was relieved to be done with them now. I needed a little brain break. There was just too much else going on. Bad sleep and poor diet had left me feeling weak and lightheaded. But no matter how hard I tried, sleep and appetite still eluded me.

I washed my cup and grabbed my keys and bag. Cassie and Dray would be home later tonight, and I would head back home after work. I had no idea what to expect, but since I'd initiated the last disastrous conversation, I would wait for Nix to start it this time.

Clutch was also never one to pry. I could only assume he knew what was going on because he and Nix spoke often. He hadn't said anything to me except that if I needed to talk, he was there. One thing was certain, Nix and I could not have asked for a better set of friends.

The true heat of summer had found its way to Los Angeles, and even early in the morning, warmth and light radiated off the sidewalks, streets and cars. I'd found a way to Clutch's shop that was sort of roundabout, but I managed to avoid the morning traffic by going a few miles out of my way. The road traveled along the base of the San Gabriel Mountains and through a few quiet streets that bordered a ravine, which had been carved by rain runoff. It was a far more scenic route than the freeway. The houses were large, old manses with manicured lawns and massive trees that had to have been growing there since the early part of the twentieth century.

I turned on the radio, and naturally, the first song was Tom Petty's "Free Falling". It was exactly how I'd felt for the past few weeks, ever since Nana's death. The ground wasn't solid under my feet. And it wasn't all due to problems with Nix or the proposal or the bad feelings between us. Nana's death had triggered some emotions that I'd buried for the sake of my sanity, a sanity that sometimes seemed more fragile than I realized. Every time my words slipped away and talking became a chore, I worried that I was going to fall back into my muted state, and this time, I was sure I wouldn't find my way back.

My dusty windshield made the sunlight extra harsh. I kept my eyes on the road and reached into the console to feel for my sunglasses. My fingers never made contact with them, so I pulled down the visor. I'd reached the stretch of road that was lined by hills on one side and an empty stretch of land on the other.

The sun was still low enough that the visor was useless. I glanced down into the console for just a second, and when I lifted my eyes, a coyote was standing in the road. It froze. I yanked the steering wheel hard to avoid it. The bottom of my car scraped the rough edge of asphalt as my front tires dove off the road. My head spun, and the sensation of falling down a cliff took hold of me. I gripped the wheel as the metal, glass and human screams twisted together. I let go of the steering wheel and covered my ears to stop the horrid noise, but it didn't stop. It was in my head. My mom's scream was the worst. "My babies!" she cried. "Please, God, spare my babies!" I covered my face to stop the images, the sight of my dad's face, dead and pale, staring out the front windshield just as he had moments before when the deer had crossed our path. The radio blasted a commercial for car insurance, and I lowered my hands. My car had rolled off the road only several feet and stopped hard on a lamppost. A cloud of dust swirled around me. There was no sign of the coyote.

My throat was dry and my hands shook wildly. My car was still running. I put it in reverse and pressed the gas, but it was stuck on something. I opened the door and got out, keeping my hand against the car for support. The light post was on a cement pedestal and my front bumper was wedged on top of it. I glanced back at the road, and my heart rate sped up and my breathing felt labored. I wasn't completely sure that I would have been able to drive even if the car was free.

I sat in the front seat and pressed my arm against my stomach to keep from throwing up. I reached into my bag for my phone. I wasn't completely sure if words would come out, but I dialed Nix. It rang several times and went to voicemail. "Hey, Nix." My voice sounded strange and forced. "I need you." I broke down into sobs and hung up. I replayed my words in my fuzzy mind and realized it was the kind of message that would make anyone freak out. I called back and hoped to hell he would answer this time. "Hey, Nix, I'm all right, but I had an accident and the car won't move." I couldn't stop myself from sniffling into the phone. "Call me when you hear this."

I hung up and held the phone against my chest, hoping he would call back soon. The sun was pouring through the windshield. My coyote friend trotted across the field, smiling back at me as if he knew he'd caused the wreck.

A car pulled over and honked. "Everything all right?" a woman called through the open window on the passenger's side.

I leaned out and waved. "I'm fine."

It had only been a fender bender, and I felt no physical pain, but as I sat there, my nausea and dizziness intensified and a cold sweat broke out on my skin. Shock. It seemed my classes were coming in handy.

I reached into my overnight bag and pulled out my sweatshirt. It was at least eighty degrees outside and the inside of the car was even warmer, but I was shivering. I wrapped myself in the sweatshirt, lowered the seat back and closed my eyes. Forcing myself to relax only made me more tense. It was only the anxiety caused by the accident and nothing more, I told myself. For years I'd hated driving in cars, and a panic attack would usually take over on long car trips. Learning to drive hadn't been easy, but once I'd felt secure behind the wheel, I'd realized the personal freedom that came with it, especially in Los Angeles where driving was like breathing, a necessity of life, I'd pushed my fears down. But I'd never felt completely comfortable behind the wheel, and now, I feared this would set me back further.

I lifted the phone in my hand to make sure it had service. All the bars were there, but Nix hadn't called. I didn't know what to think of it. My hands were still shaky, but lowering my head back had helped with the dizziness and nausea.

Clutch answered on the first ring.

"Hey, Scottie, are you almost here?"

The sound of his voice brought instant tears. I sniffled a few times before I could speak.

"Scottie? Everything all right?" It seemed I'd heard that question a million times in the past few weeks, and it suddenly dawned on me that, at the moment, nothing was all right.

"I got in a little accident."

"What? Where are you? Are you hurt?" His genuine concern made my tears flow faster.

"I'm fine, but I can't move the car. I'm sorry, Clutch. I tried to call Nix, but he didn't answer." The last words came out as a cry.

"Where are you at? I'm on my way."

***

"Scottie?" Clutch's deep voice woke me.

I sat up completely confused for a second, and then the lamppost reminded me of what had happened. My back was wet with sweat as I sat up and concentrated on getting my bearings. My limbs were still trembling, and my head felt filled with air. Clutch crouched down in the open doorway. His head still reached the top of the car.

The look of worry on his face made me put my hand on his arm. "I'm not hurt. Just a little out of it, that's all."

He stood back up and cast a big shadow over the car. He walked to the lamppost and crouched down again to see where the car was lodged. "Tore your bumper halfway off, but I can get you loose. Turn on the car and put it in neutral. And take off the emergency brake."

It took me a second to sort out his directions. Once the car was in neutral, he reached down under it and lifted the dangling bumper up hard. Metal scraped cement, and I gasped as the car rolled backwards, now free of the pedestal.

He walked back to the car and leaned down to the window. "It'll drive fine. Follow me back to the shop, and I can fix that bumper."

I took a deep breath and forced a smile. "All right."

His long blond hair bounced on his confident shoulders as he returned to his car and climbed in. He pulled out onto the road. I put the car in drive and my fingers tightened around the steering wheel. My breathing grew shallow, and it seemed my pulse was thrumming in my ears. My foot was frozen to the brake pedal. I couldn't move. The thought of pulling out onto the road was terrifying. Clutch's car had disappeared around the first curve. Tears spilled down my cheeks. I sat there for several more minutes trying to convince myself that I could do this, that I just needed a few deep breaths to relax, but my foot was glued to the brake. A few minutes later, Clutch's car came back around the curve, and he pulled off the road next to me.

I was completely embarrassed. I just wanted to sink into a puddle and be evaporated quickly by the hot sun. He got out and opened my car door. My shoulders shook as he lowered his hand for me to take. My legs were like wet noodles under me. He put his arm around my waist to keep me upright as he walked me to his car.

He didn't say a word as he opened the car door. He held my arm as I lowered myself onto the passenger seat. The temperature outside was rising rapidly, but I pulled my sweatshirt tight around me and ground myself deep into the bucket seat. Shame heated my face, but I couldn't con-

97

vince myself to pull out of my funk. The accident, the silly little accident, had triggered so many emotions, I couldn't tame any of them into a coherent feeling. And my phone remained silent. Nix hadn't even bothered to call back. I'd pushed away the most important and most solid part of my life, and now, when I needed him, he wasn't there.

"I'll have someone drive me back here to pick up your car. Don't worry about it. Do you want me to take you home?"

I shook my head. My fingers curled. I wanted a pen and paper. I closed my eyes and swallowed. *Talk damnit.* "I'll work." The words popped out, but it had taken every ounce of my energy to utter them.

Clutch was driving far slower than normal, almost as if he worried I'd jump from the car if he sped up. And I wasn't convinced that I wouldn't. Everything I'd gone through to bolster my confidence in a car had been rendered useless with just one stupid little accident. I hadn't felt despair like this for a long time, and I couldn't see any way out of the darkness.

Chapter 13

Nix

I finished up my last tattoo of the morning and gladly sent my fidgety client on his way. Stormy had been working for three hours on an elaborate dragon tattoo, but she, too, was finishing up. I'd let the store calls go to voicemail, and now there was a string of messages to listen to. Cassie was the glue that kept things together. It would take her several days to restore Freefall back to a smooth operation.

I'd thought of nothing but Scotlyn all morning, hell, all week. I decided to take a break and call her. My cell phone wasn't on the counter. I walked into my office. It wasn't there either. My mind was so screwed up lately, I couldn't even remember where I'd laid my damn phone. I walked into the small room where Stormy was working.

I glanced over her shoulder. "That looks awesome, Stormy."

She tilted her head to admire her artwork. "Thanks."

"Hey, did you happen to see my phone?"

"Yeah." She looked toward the counter. "You left it in here. I had to turn off the ringer. It kept going off and startling him." She motioned to her client on the table, and he shrugged, slightly embarrassed, in response.

In two steps, I was at the counter. There were three voicemails and four texts. I looked over at Stormy who was cleaning up the tattoo. "You might have mentioned that the phone was ringing," I said sharply.

She peered up at me looking completely unfazed by my angry tone. "Guess you should remember to keep it with you," she shot back.

I was pissed, but I was more worried about the messages I'd missed. I walked out of the room and dialed up my voicemail. The first two were from Scotlyn about an accident. My chest tightened at the sound of her trembling voice. The third was from Clutch.

"Nix, where the fuck are you? I've been texting. You need to call me as soon as you get this."

My heart was slamming against my ribs as I dialed Clutch. He answered on the first ring.

"Dude, where are you at?"

"I'm at Freefall. What's going on? Where's Scotlyn?"

"I'm going to walk out back," he'd dropped his voice low. I heard the back door to his shop open and shut, and a motor was running somewhere behind the building. "Scotlyn is sitting on the picnic table out in front of the shop drinking a soda. She's not hurt."

"Goddamn, Clutch, you just about gave me a heart attack."

"She's not hurt physically," he continued, before I could berate him further. "There was a coyote on the street, and she swerved to miss it. Her car went off the road and rolled down a small incline, stopping against a light pole. The fender was dislodged, but that's about it."

"That's good to hear."

"When her family died, didn't you tell me her father was trying not to hit an animal?"

"Yeah, a deer. He lost control of the car and went off the side of the—" My head had been like Swiss cheese, and now the holes were filling in. "Fuck."

"She's been sort of vegging out and not talking to any of us. I asked her what kind of coffee she wanted from the coffee shop, and she wrote it down on a sticky note and handed it to me."

"Aw shit." My heartbeat slowed, and it felt as if someone was pressing down on my chest.

"You need to get over here."

"I'm on my way."

***

I'd dialed Scotlyn's phone three times, but it went straight to voicemail as if she'd turned it off. Traffic was always gnarly when I needed to get somewhere, and today was no exception to that rule. I smacked the damn steering wheel hard, but surprisingly, it didn't make the cars go any faster. I kept my phone nearby, assuming that if things got worse, Clutch would call me.

I was pissed as hell at Stormy, not as much for turning down the phone without letting me know it had rang, but for her bitchy response. It had me wondering if she was worth keeping on.

I was just ten minutes from the shop when my phone

rang. I was hoping like hell it was Scotlyn. It was Clutch.

I tapped the screen and Clutch's voice came through the speakers. "Nix, uh, we've got a problem." Clutch sounding stressed happened about as often as a snowstorm in L.A..

"Shit, just put her on the phone. I need to talk to her even if she won't speak back."

He paused. "That's the problem. I'm not sure where she is."

"What?"

"She was sitting out front with her soda. Her car is still in the garage being fixed. So she took off on foot somewhere."

"Sonavabitch. She couldn't have gotten far. How long ago did she leave?"

"I'm sorry, bro, I'm not sure. I got busy with work and—"

"No, it's not your fault. I'm almost there. See you in a few." The butt of my hand smacked the steering wheel again. I had no idea what state she'd left in, but from what Clutch had said, she was pretty out of it.

My tires chirped as I hit the parking lot in front of Clutch's shop at full speed. He met me out front. "Dude, I'm real sorry. She was sitting right here sipping soda. Mike was in back working on a car, and I was in the office. Mike said he saw her sitting at her computer for a few minutes and then she walked out again. Her purse is gone. I walked down to the donut shop, but she wasn't there. Everything else along here is just industrial buildings."

I glanced around the area and then looked back at Clutch. "You said she wasn't talking."

He combed his hair back with his fingers and stared down at the ground, as if trying to figure out what to say next. "Nix, she looked really bad. Pale and skinny, like she hasn't eaten in a week. She couldn't drive the car, so I gave her a ride. She sort of just curled up into a ball in the front seat. She didn't say anything after that."

I shook my head. "This is my fault. She was trying to make up, and I blew her off because I thought she didn't trust me. My stupid fucking ego got in the way."

"Beating yourself up right now isn't going to find her," Clutch said.

"If anything happens to her—" My words broke off. I looked up at Clutch. "She's my life."

His face brightened with an idea. "The computer. We can check her history and see if she was looking something up. Maybe we can figure out where she went."

We walked inside. My gut was knotted with worry. Clutch plunked on the keyboard and pulled down her history. "Yep, here's something. Sierra Madre Cemetery."

"Sierra Madre? That's where her family is buried. She told me someday she would work up enough courage to visit. She was in the hospital recovering when they were buried."

Clutch leaned into the back room. "Hey, Mike, the buses that stop on Hill Street, where do they usually head?"

"East." he answered back.

Clutch rolled his eyes. "All right, can you be more specific? Would the route go as far as Sierra Madre?"

"Yeah, I think so."

Clutch looked at me. "Get the address off the computer.

103

Do you want me to come with you?"

"No, thanks."

Clutch nodded. "Yeah, it needs to be just you."

CHAPTER 14

Nix

It was late afternoon by the time I'd slogged my way back through the long stretches of traffic. The sun was still high enough in the summer sky to keep the temperature stifling hot. Even with the snarls of gridlock dotting the entire Los Angeles freeway system, I was certain I'd made it to the cemetery long before Scotlyn's bus would arrive.

The bus bench was a half mile from the cemetery entrance. If we were wrong about where she'd headed, then I'd just wasted an hour that I could have spent looking for her. She was still not answering her phone. All I could do was hope that our detective work would pay off. Scotlyn was sensible and much stronger than she allowed herself to believe, but my innate sense to protect her and keep her safe from harm had kicked in. I was wound tight, and I wouldn't relax until I knew Scotlyn was all right.

I parked in a small turnout just inside of the cemetery, making sure to hide my car behind a copse of oak trees. I didn't want her to see me. If she'd made this trip to see her family, she obviously needed this time alone with them.

About half an hour passed. Clutch texted. "Have you found her?"

TESS OLIVER

"Not yet," I texted back. My gut was telling me she would show. The accident had stirred up the horror of that nightmarish day when she'd lost everyone she cared about. It made sense that she would want to come here. Even with the months of therapy and passing of time, she still occasionally woke in the middle of the night gasping for air and shaking from a bad dream. It was hard as hell to watch. Usually, on those nights, once I folded her into my arms, she'd settle down, the trembling would subside and she'd fall back asleep. I wasn't sure if it would be enough this time. I wasn't sure if I would be enough. My confidence in this relationship had been shaky since the proposal.

The distinct sound of a bus engine rattled the windows of my car. I could see the gleaming top of the bus over the hedge surrounding the cemetery. I waited, hoping I'd see her come around the corner soon. If I didn't, then I was lost about where to go next, and that thought scared the shit out of me.

Then I saw her. She looked frail, and as if some life had been washed out of her. I had to keep myself from jumping out of the car to pull her into my arms. She was holding a bouquet of daisies that looked slightly wilted from the bus ride. She walked into the mortuary office and then came back out with a map. For a moment, I wondered if I should show myself, if I should join her in this. But I knew Scotlyn well enough to know that this was a highly personal moment. This was something she needed to do alone.

I sent a text to Clutch. "I found her."

She hiked along the long, curvy road and walked across the manicured lawn and around the maze of headstones, finally stopping near an ornate wrought iron bench. She stood for a few minutes before dropping to her knees in front of several headstones.

Watching her, the girl who owned my heart and my soul, sit alone on the grass, her shoulders shaking and her head bowed in anguish was one of the hardest things I'd ever done. After twenty minutes, I couldn't keep myself in the car any longer.

I traveled along the same road. She hadn't seen me yet, and I had no idea how she'd react. She pushed to her feet and placed some daisies into the small cup holders on each grave. I waited for her to finish. So many words had flown through my head in the past few minutes that I still had no idea what I would say. Then, she turned around, and all the words fell into place.

She stared at me for a second as if she was looking at a mirage.

"Scotlyn, hope you don't mind. I just needed to know you were safe."

Her vivid blue eyes were misted from crying. She looked sadder than I'd ever seen her. She looked back at the headstones and the flimsy stems of yellow and white daisies. She continued to stare down at them. "He won't be there to walk me down the aisle." Her quiet voice trailed up over the neatly manicured slopes. "Olivia, my maid of honor, can't hold my bouquet." She sobbed once. "And I won't hear my mom sniffling into her handkerchief while I say vows." She smiled weakly. "Mom used to cry during greeting card commercials." She reached up and wiped away a tear. "I guess that's where I get it from. I can't get married because they won't be there."

I swallowed hard. It had never occurred to me that the

notion of getting married would just be a painful reminder of how much she'd lost. "I don't need a damn certificate or ring to know that you are my life. I don't pretend to know what this is like." I waved my hands toward the headstones. "I know that there is a piece of you that can never be mended. And all I can do is be there for you when that pain takes hold. And I know it does...a lot. I see it in your face, that incredible face that I can never stop thinking about." I dropped my gaze for a second to catch my breath. She looked so vulnerable, so distraught that it was tearing me up inside. I peered up at her. She stared back at me with glossy eyes. I was having a damn hard time keeping it together. "I can't promise you that nothing will ever happen to me, just like you can't make that promise to me. I have everything I could want right now, a thriving business, good friends, a house of my own, but none of it matters without you, Scotlyn. Three years ago I found a picture of a girl." I smiled. "Actually, the picture found me. It was stuck to my shoe." Her lip turned up, and that tiny gesture helped prod me forward. "It was only a crumpled up picture, but it stayed tucked in my wallet. That day, you curled yourself around my heart. And you're still there. My feelings are so strong for you, Scotlyn, the word love doesn't even cover it." I stepped closer. She still hadn't said a word. "I can't lose you." My voice wavered. "I can't fucking lose you, baby."

Her long lashes fluttered down. I lunged forward and caught her before she collapsed to the ground. I lifted her into my arms. "Let me take you home, Scotlyn."

She snuggled against me. "I am home."

CHAPTER 15

Scotlyn

The aroma of smoky butter drifted through the air as the shadows of dusk splashed their usual artwork on the kitchen walls. I took another bite of the grilled cheese sandwich that Nix had made me. It was burned black on one side and nearly cold on the other, but it was the best grilled cheese I'd ever eaten.

The fading light played its usual tricks on the ever changing color in Nix's eyes, but gold specks sparkled as he smiled down at the sandwich on my plate. "It's a good thing I earn a living with a tattoo gun instead of a spatula."

"It's delicious." I took another bite and drank some of the milk he'd poured me.

He reached across and wiped away the milk moustache with his thumb. "Why don't we take the day off tomorrow? Just hang out here, you know? Celebrate your end of finals."

"That actually sounds really good. What about my poor smashed car?"

"Clutch already took care of it." I smiled. "I've never seen him so freaked out."

I sighed. "I'll have to call him later. I didn't mean to scare him...or you. I just wasn't thinking straight, and suddenly, I had an overwhelming urge to visit my family. Hope you can forgive me."

"There's nothing to forgive, baby. The only thing that matters is that you're here with me now."

The past weeks had been so hard. It had felt as if Nix and I were coming apart at the seam that we'd sewn so tightly shut between us. Nix had never been a stranger to me. Almost from the start, I'd felt deeply connected to him. Sitting with him in our cozy kitchen seemed so familiar and right, the raw edges of the past few weeks seemed to smooth away. I was sitting with the man I loved.

I sniffled and pressed my napkin to my nose. It seemed I'd spent more time in tears than with dry eyes lately. "Thank you, Nix, for being my family. For the longest time, the loneliness felt like quicksand, a deep hole that I was never going to escape from and that would eventually consume me. You saved me from that despair, and I'll never forget that."

"I think that picture found me for a reason." He dropped his gaze. Moments of shyness were rare for Nix. "These past few weeks have been torture." He lifted his eyes. "I'm sorry my big bloated head got in the way of things."

"No, it wasn't your bloated head. It was bad communication from both sides. I promise to work on that."

"Me too." He cleared his throat. "Well, I'm going to go in and take a shower. Do you want to watch a movie?"

"Sounds good."

I'd nibbled longer on my sandwich, knowing that hunger had played a part in the emotion filled day. The minor accident would have been hardly a blip in most people's routine, but I wasn't most people. The terrible coincidence of swerving to avoid an animal and rolling off the road had shaken me severely. My family's accident had come back to me in painful splashes. And then, as I sat outside of Clutch's shop wondering how everything had gone so terribly wrong, I was suddenly overwhelmed by guilt. I had never gone to their gravesites. It was fear and anguish and every other wretched emotion that'd kept me from going. Now, I was glad I'd gone. As hard as it was seeing their names, Scott James, Lynne James and Olivia James etched into the stone grave markers, it gave me a tiny sense of closure, something I'd missed out on. In a way, I envied that they'd all left this earth together, and there were still times that I questioned why I'd gotten stuck here without them. Then I saw Nix standing there in the cemetery, and the ground immediately felt more solid beneath my feet. My family was gone, but I was no longer alone.

The shower was still running as I placed my plate in the sink. I walked through the bedroom and pushed open the bathroom door. Soapy steam puffed around me in clouds. Nix's naked body showed through the mottled glass of the shower. I stripped off my clothes and bra and panties. His face popped up from the spray of water as I opened the glass door. His eyes drifted down over my naked body. Then he lifted his amber gaze to my face. It seemed his fists curled against his desire to grab me. It was sweet and a little frustrating all at the same time.

I stepped under the hot streams of water and pressed my body against his. He hesitated but only for a brief second. My hands went behind his neck, and his arms went around me. It was a kiss that had been on the edge of our minds the past few weeks, but we'd both held it back. I'd been the cause of that. The proposal, Nana's death, the horrid series of miscommunications had kept us from each other's arms. But that was over.

My hands smoothed over the hard muscles of his shoulders and back as his hungry mouth traveled from my lips down my neck to my breasts. My nipples puckered as his tongue stroked my wet skin. His rock hard erection pressed against my belly. I wrapped my fingers around it. Nix's deep voice rumbled off the tile walls. "God, baby, I've missed touching you." He pressed his mouth against my ear as his fingers slid down my back. His hands went around my naked bottom and he lifted me. My legs wrapped around his waist as he braced me against the steamy wall of the shower. My fingers wrapped into his wet hair as he pushed inside of me. A small cry popped from my mouth as he drove himself deeper. Sandwiched between his strong body and the hard wall, I found the leverage I needed to grind my swollen clit against him. He rocked against me, and my fingers wrapped tighter in his hair. In my delirium, my eyes opened just long enough to catch the intensity of his deep amber gaze. It assured me how much I belonged in his arms.

His movements deepened and I sucked in a gulp of warm, soap-scented air as my pussy clenched around him. "Nix, yes, please." My quiet plea was drowned out by the steady streams of water, but he held me tighter and continued to drive into me, holding me tightly over him.

His head dropped back and his body shuddered against me as he came. Slowly, I lowered my legs down and melted against him. Nix was my solid. He was the person to show me how to find the ground when my feet were dangling above it. His arms wrapped around me. Warm water ran in steady streams down our naked skin. I could have stood there all day.

Chapter 16

Nix

"Hungry?" I patted my stomach. "Don't know about you, but this make-up sex stuff can really rouse a sleepy appetite."

Scotlyn leaned up on her elbow and traced circles on my chest with her fingernails. "This might sound shocking, but I have a hankering for another one of your half-charred, half-uncooked grilled cheese sandwiches."

"That is my specialty. Two hybrid grilled cheese sandwiches coming right up." I reached up and placed my hand behind her head to lower her mouth to mine. Her soft, lush lips parted as she kissed me. I was hard again. "Just as soon as I can pull myself away from you," I muttered against her mouth. I twisted to my side and my hands took hold of her waist. I tugged her toward me and her long thighs straddled my body. Her long lashes shadowed her blue eyes as she braced her hands against my chest and slid down over my cock. Her blonde hair flowed over her shoulders and I watched her face as her hot, wet pussy took in every inch of me.

She felt thin and fragile beneath my fingers, as if I could easily break her. Scotlyn's silky body slipped up and down through my grasp until a pink blush covered her skin. A soft sound drifted from her throat as she climaxed. She dropped her hands onto the mattress on each side of my face and braced herself as I slammed into her again and again.

"Harder, baby," she whispered. "Harder."

I grabbed hold of her and rolled her onto her back. Long, satiny thighs tightened around my waist as I slid inside of her again. The headboard smacked the wall, making the crease in the plaster even bigger. I grabbed her to me, nearly crushing her in my arms, as I came.

I rolled down next to her.

"I guess this is what they call making up for lost time," she said with a laugh.

"Yep, the way I've got it calculated, we'll be in this bed for about two more weeks." I turned to look at her. "Maybe no one will miss us."

She rubbed her fingertip along the stubble on my chin. "Earlier, there was mention of grilled cheese sandwiches."

"Right." I sat up. "I guess you're making up for lost food time, too. Do not know how you girls exist on air and food crumbs." I slid from bed and headed out of the room.

She laughed. "Don't you think you should put on some pants or at least some underwear?"

"Nope."

"Beware of splattering butter," she called to me.

I leaned back into the room. "Luckily for me, I've got an extremely hot and extremely naked nurse in my bed in case of any kitchen accidents." A knock rattled the door as I stepped into the front room. I didn't need to look through the peephole to know it was Dray. His knocks were easy to recognize, wild and impolite, as if he always had something important to tell me.

"Nix, it's me," he announced unnecessarily.

I opened the door and then headed to the kitchen. He stepped inside.

"Holy shit, cover that junk up. What the hell are you doing walking around in broad daylight buck fucking naked? You weren't at the shop."

I pulled the bread and cheese out of the fridge. "Nope, I'm here."

He stood in the kitchen and watched me get the supplies I needed for grilled cheese. "Yeah, I see that, and your two best friends are just swinging in the wind. Aren't you afraid of burning the little guys?"

"Who are you calling little?"

He bowed his head. "I apologize. No insult intended. I was just looking out for their welfare. Anyhow, Yosemite was very outdoorsy and pine treeish and all that shit. Cassie loves that stuff. But I prefer the beach, which reminds me— Clutch needs your part of the down payment for the beach house. I just had lunch with Rett to pick up his part of the money." Dray grabbed a slice of cheese and bread. He rubbed the bread over the butter. I pointed out the butter knife, but he dismissed the idea of using a utensil. "That guy should have a permanent weekly column in Playboy."

"Playboy only comes out once a month," I noted.

"Really? Too bad. Anyhow, he knows stuff— I didn't have a pen but—" He tapped the side of his head. "I've got it stored right up here. Going to try some new techniques, you know?"

I laughed. "And Cassie knows about these new techniques?"

"Hell no. I'm going to surprise her. I'm just embarrassed to have to learn shit like this from Rett. He's two years younger, although, his experience puts us all to shame. So have you patched things up with Scottie yet?"

"Hi, Dray," Scotlyn said from the family room. She'd pulled on a t-shirt and shorts. Her mass of blonde hair was piled up in a messy bun on her head, and, as always, my breath caught in my chest.

Dray's mouth dropped open. "Oh, hey, your car wasn't here, so I—" He kept the sandwich in his hand but backed out of the kitchen. He glanced back at me. "I guess that answers my last question. O.K. then I will be on my way." He lifted his bread and cheese to Scotlyn. "Just stopped by for some lunch." He took a bite. "Hmm, so good. Thanks, Nix." Scotlyn giggled as Dray slid out the front door.

She walked into the kitchen and pressed herself against my back. "He didn't have to leave."

"Yes, he did."

Her hands wrapped around me and smoothed over my stomach. "I think this could be a new cooking show, naked chef with rock hard abs and an amazing ass." She pinched me.

"Yeah, but I think the audience might get tired of watching me make the same thing over and over again. Grilled cheese is as far as my culinary talents reach."

"Trust me." She kissed my shoulder and the back of my neck. "No one will notice what's on the stove."

CHAPTER 17

Scotlyn

Taylor was almost giddy as she dropped the layers of white chiffon over my head. "I figured I'd catch you before we buttered ourselves with greasy suntan lotion. Now, remember, it's not finished."

"Taylor, it's all right. It's a school project. It's not like I'm here being fitted for the real thing." The silky fabric shimmied down my skin like a cream filled waterfall. "I already love the way it feels." The dress was strapless and had a slim line with a corset style closure in the back The asymmetrical bodice draped across my waist and ended in a small cluster of glimmering beads.

Cassie stepped in front of the coffee table where I was standing. "Oh my gosh, Taylor, this is amazing. The craftsmanship is outrageous."

Taylor beamed as she fussed with the long folds on the train. "It helps to have a beautiful model."

"No, Taylor, really." I glanced down at the shimmering dress. It moved like buttery silk around my legs. "You are a genius. I feel like I'm in a fairytale. This bodice reminds me of my mom's wedding dress. She had it covered up with one of those dry cleaning bags, and every once in awhile, my sister and I would sneak into her closet and unzip the bag." Since the visit to the cemetery, I'd been reminiscing a lot about my childhood. They had been years to cherish, and thinking about that time seemed to help me cope when I was feeling blue.

"Where is the dress now?" Taylor asked.

I shook my head. "Gone with everything else. My aunt held an estate sale while I was in the hospital. She'd said she needed the money to pay for my upkeep. She made it sound like I was a piece of livestock. And, apparently, she thought I'd be eating her out of house and home because it wasn't for clothing and shoes. She only went to second hand stores." I ran my fingers over the perfectly sewn ripples on the bodice. "This is just exquisite, Taylor."

Deep voices rolled up from the cement bike path in front of the rental house. Cassie scurried to the window. "Phew, it's not the guys."

Taylor and I looked at her questioningly.

She lifted her hands. "What? It's bad luck to see the bride in her gown before the wedding."

I laughed. "Yes, but I think there has to be an actual wedding planned for that to be a problem."

Cassie shrugged. "You can't be too careful."

Taylor walked around and pinned the parts that needed altering. I'd gained back some of the weight I'd lost, but my measurements were still off.

"When do you have to turn this project in?" I asked.

"In September, when classes start again. This is such a big project it stretches across two quarters. They give us all summer to work on it."

"Well, you are simply amazing, Taylor," I said. "I can't wait to buy your label when it hits the stores. Which it will."

"That would be so cool to see my stuff on actual people instead of just headless dress dummies. Well, that should do for the first fitting. Cass, help me get this off of Scottie and then let's head out to the beach."

I put on my suit while Cassie and Taylor filled up the 'girls only' ice chest. Cassie and I had each brought an ice chest, and we'd decided to put them both to use. Normally, the guys guzzled the drinks and food so fast, we girls were lucky to get a baggie or Tupperware with crumbs left behind. And what the guys considered acceptable beach food was quite different from what we girls craved while sitting in skimpy suits on blazing hot sand.

Cassie had written the words 'girls only' on a piece of paper and taped it to the top of the ice chest. "I already dragged the other chest down to the towels, figuring they'd be wanting something soon," Cassie said.

Taylor and I each took a handle, and we carried it, like a little kid swinging between us, down to the patch of sand where our beach chairs had already been planted.

Clutch's head stuck up above the rest as the three men waited for a wave. They'd gotten up at the crack of dawn to surf, but in the afternoon, the on-shore wind and droves of swimmers made surfing impossible. The afternoon was for body surfing.

"I can already see Dray's sunburn from here," Cassie said. "The lotion is supposed to be waterproof, but I don't know if the manufacturer takes into consideration men who spend more time in the water than on the sand. You'd think after surfing for three hours this morning that they'd be bored of salt and seaweed and other icky, floating things."

Taylor leaned into the ice chest and pulled out the grapes. "Hey, when are Rett and Finley coming?"

"Tonight," Cassie put out her palm for a clump of grapes. She popped one into her mouth. "Ooh, these are good."

"How did the article go?" I asked. "Are they getting donations?"

Cassie plucked off another grape. "Finley said the pictures are drawing a lot of attention, and I guess they're doing well enough to hire on another full-time worker. That's the only way they were able to get a few free days to come down here." She reached into the ice chest and pulled out a baggie filled with cherry tomatoes. "This whole gender specific ice chest thing is friggin' brilliant."

Taylor glanced over at the ice chest near the towels the guys had laid out. She nearly fell back in her chair with laughter. "I thought it would say 'boys only'."

I rose up in my chair and read the paper taped to the top of the chest. It read 'Neanderthal grub'. And Cassie had embellished the sign with a picture of a caveman eating a giant piece of meat.

"Speaking of the knuckle draggers," Cassie quipped. "They finally got tired of the water." She shook her head. "Look at that man of mine walking in those flippers. What a dork." Cassie complained and made fun of Dray constantly, but she'd fallen in love with him the first moment she'd met him. And as different as they were, they were absolutely perfect for each other.

Clutch was the first to reach us. He dropped his fins

into the sand and stared down at the 'girls only' ice chest. "What's this shit?" he asked.

Taylor pointed to the other chest. "That one is for you guys." Dray and Nix reached us too. After our rough patch, Nix and I had been flirting and having wild sex as if our relationship had just started. Frankly, I was hoping things would stay that way. He slipped me a 'for my eyes only' smile as he followed Clutch to their ice chest. They all stared down at the top of it. Nix laughed.

Clutch leaned down to open it. "Then there better be some wooly mammoth steaks and brontosaurus sized drumsticks inside."

Dray lifted his towel to shake off the sand, and the three of us lifted our arms to avoid grit pelting our faces.

"Oh my gosh." Cassie leaned forward in her chair. "I'm going in the water to wash off."

Taylor hopped up, too. "Come on, Scottie. It's too hot on the sand anyhow."

Clutch stared up at us with half his sandwich already devoured. "Was it something we said?"

Dray waved us on as he grabbed a sandwich. "That's right, wiggle on down to the water so we can watch you girls strutting your stuff while we eat our caveman lunch. Later, I might drag you by the hair to our cave," he called to Cassie, earning himself some nasty looking glares from the two women sitting nearby.

Dray raised up his hands. "What? She loves it." The women returned their attention to their books.

Taylor plowed right into the waves, but Cassie and I preferred to take the cowardly layered approach, getting a few more inches wet each time, until, eventually, with any luck, we were submerged to our hips. The water always seemed much colder when the air was excessively hot.

Taylor swam out farther, but Cassie and I stayed closer to shore, swaying with the constant motion of the current. Two guys were boogie boarding nearby. One was already trying to start a conversation with Taylor. It seemed she was happy to engage in conversation if it meant a chance to try his boogie board.

"She is so talented," I said. "That dress felt like I was wearing gossamer."

"It looked absolutely gorgeous on you." Cassie's bottom lip twisted, and I knew what was coming next. "Have you guys talked about the proposal again?"

A small wave slapped us both on the back, but we kept on our feet. "No, we haven't." The disappointment in my tone shocked me. "Nix seems to understand. That day when I went to the cemetery to visit my family, I realized that they were the reason the proposal seemed so daunting to me."

Cassie looked confused. "I thought it was because the call about Nana came at the same time?"

"That just added to it, and it sort of kept me from figuring out why I was feeling so down about something that should have sent me over the moon." I lifted my feet and floated onto my back. Cassie joined me.

"You don't have any family to attend, no dad to walk you down the aisle or sister to stand next to you." Cassie was always incredibly astute.

A bigger wave pushed us up and we laughed.

"Hey, Scottie, if you ever decide to get married, I know

I can't take your sister's place, but I'd be thrilled to stand next to you, you know, hold your bouquet and straighten your train and all that important stuff."

I pushed my feet down to the sandy bottom. Cassie stood too.

I reached over and hugged her. "I will hold you to that, my friend."

We glanced toward the sand. Dray had his head and shoulders buried inside the ice chest. I laughed. "Maybe he thinks there's a secret bottom where we stored all the really good stuff."

Chapter 18

Nix

Dray rolled his face my direction without lifting his head from the chair. "Hey, Nix, check out the 'girls only' ice chest. We're down to empty baggies and balls of foil in ours."

"You kidding? Cassie probably has the fucking thing booby trapped."

"Oh, come one, you coward." Dray leaned forward and looked over at Clutch. His long legs were stretched out in front of the beach chair, yet, he looked anything but relaxed. "Hey, Clutch," Dray started but Clutch shook his head without pulling his attention from the water. "I'm not hungry anymore," Clutch said.

Dray and I snapped our faces toward each other. "Did he just say he wasn't hungry?" I looked at Clutch and then followed his line of vision down to the water. Taylor had borrowed some guy's boogie board. She was flying over a nice little curl.

"She's pretty good," I said.

"Uh huh," Clutch answered.

"What the hell is your deal? She's just using her cuteness to get a couple of free rides on a boogie board," Dray said.

"Yep," Clutch answered in another terse, clipped response.

"Anyhow," Dray continued, "I tried some of the stuff Rett was telling me about, but Cassie was having none of it."

I raised a brow, wondering if I should ask for further details and then thought better of it. "Maybe you were just doing it wrong."

"Thanks for the vote of confidence. No, I think I was doing it just fine. Although, I do believe that our boy, Rett, was born with the Midas touch. Right, Clutch?" He looked over at Clutch, who, just like the guards in front of Buckingham Palace, hadn't flinched from his sentry position in the beach chair.

Even with the sea breeze, it was in the nineties on the sand. A lot of people, and even most of the seagulls, had migrated to the water. Cassie and Scotlyn had stayed closer to shore, letting the current take them out and push them back in, while still holding a conversation. Taylor was definitely enjoying herself with her two new boogie boarding buddies. Sometimes it seemed she went out of her way to keep Clutch focused on her. She was nineteen, and it was always obvious that she straddled the fence between her teen and her adult years. Her fairly transparent plan to garner Clutch's attention had definitely worked. As hot as the temperature was, it was like ice compared to the glowing heat of rage circulating around my friend.

"Dude, she knows what she's doing," I said. "Just relax. We're on vacation, remember?"

Clutch had on dark sunglasses but I could sense his eye roll behind the dark lenses. "This from my friend who basically had his briefs wadded up inside his ass because he and his girlfriend were having problems."

I put my hand up to let him know I got the message. "You're right. I'll just shut the hell up."

Dray got up and stretched out on his stomach. "Think I'll work on my back tan."

"Yeah, it should go nicely with the blistering sunburn that's already there," I said.

The chair next to me squeaked as Clutch sat forward. One of the guys with Taylor took hold of her waist as she pulled herself onto the boogie board. Sand, chair and anything else in his path popped up in the air as Clutch thundered across the beach toward the water.

"Uh oh."

Dray twisted around to take a look.

I sat forward. "This should be entertaining."

Taylor glanced toward shore and saw Clutch storming toward her like Poseidon marching back to the sea. "All he needs is a fucking trident in his fist, and all the sea creatures would be surfacing to behold him," I said.

Dray turned around and sat up for a better view. Taylor pointed out Clutch to the two guys on the boogie boards. Even from the distance we sat, it was easy to see their eyes bug out and their mouths drop open. They hopped up on their boards and paddled away like two fish trying to outrun a shark.

Dray burst out laughing.

I shook my head. "Fucking classic." I got up. "Well, it's

hot as hell out here, so I think I'm going to join the girls in the water."

Dray got up and followed.

I waded toward Scotlyn, and she shrieked as I dove under and headed straight for her. I grabbed her around the waist and shot out of the water with her over my shoulder.

She smacked my shoulder. "Stop, my suit is falling off!"

"That's part of the plan." I swung her off my shoulder and rolled her down to my arms.

She wrapped her arms around my neck and stretched her long legs out. "This is better. Much more dignified."

I drew my gaze along her body. Water splashed over her creamy skin, causing the fabric of her bikini to cling to her breasts. Her nipples pressed against the soft cotton. "You would make an extremely hot mermaid." I wanted nothing more than to carry her up to shore and into the house.

She kicked her feet in the surf. "Yes, as long as you consider a fish tail to be erotic."

I thought about that scenario. "Yeah. No. No, I don't. I prefer legs. Especially this pair, right here."

She peered up at me, and I leaned down and kissed her lightly on the mouth. We'd smoothed things out a few weeks ago but the rounds of make-up sex hadn't ended. As far as I was concerned, they could continue until the end of time.

"Hey," I said, "let's take a drive tonight. About ten miles along Pacific Coast Highway, there's a quiet little beach that takes a bit of a hike along rocks to get to. It's crowded with surfers in the morning, but at night…"

"We can have it all to ourselves?" The gleam in her eye

assured me that she'd caught my meaning, which probably didn't take too much of an imagination stretch since alone time with her had been at the top of my priority list this whole trip. But a crowded beach house didn't make that an easy task.

"If we're lucky. We can bring some blankets and—"

She lifted up and kissed me this time. "Hey, buddy, I need no further convincing. It's a date."

Chapter 19

Scotlyn

The rest of the group barbecued steaks and hung out at the house to wait for Finley and Rett. Nix and I climbed into his car with two blankets and a bottle of wine. It was great spending time with everyone. It had become a tradition I looked forward to each summer, but this particular summer was different. Nix and I had gone through the first real trial of our relationship, and we'd come out the other side closer than ever. For the moment, keeping our hands off each other was not an option.

A half moon painted a long strip of gold across the black water below. The beach was more of a cove, bordered on both sides by the cliffs. Nix pulled the car onto a turnout and parked. I looked through the window. There was a narrow, somewhat treacherous looking path leading down to the sand.

I glanced down at my dress and sandals. I was dressed for a fun and fast flirt on the beach but not a rocky hike. "Before we left the house, I was sure I'd made a brilliant clothing choice. Now I'm not so sure. I should have worn shorts and my hiking boots."

Nix's gaze flickered down, and a smile tilted his mouth.

He reached over and slid the hem of my sundress up high on my thigh, his calloused fingertips making contact with my skin the entire length. He leaned over and pressed his warm mouth against my leg. His kisses continued up toward my panties. Heat rushed between my legs, and my entire body reacted to his mouth.

"No," I sputtered between short breaths, "the dress was the way to go."

He lifted his face and the hunger in it mirrored the way I felt. "Just hang on to me, and you'll be fine." He opened his door and then turned back. "But I'm not making any promises once we hit the sand." We stepped out of the car and a tangy breeze shot up from the water. The willowy skirt of my dressed billowed up like a parachute.

Nix laughed as I struggled to push it down. "I'm just going to be pushing it up again." He took the blankets under his arm and the wine in one hand and I held his shoulders. Having traveled the path before with his surfboard, he seemed to know right where to put his feet. Sandals made it tough, but I followed his footprints. We made it down to the beach in one piece. And it was worth the hike. The sand glowed ivory white in the moonlight, and, aside from a small group of gulls huddled near the water, we were completely alone.

"Thank you for thinking of this." I peered up at the jagged cliff tops that stuck out over the sand. The highway was far enough away that the waves drowned out any car motors. It was as if we were standing alone on our own planet with no other humans around. "This place is amazing."

Nix dropped the blankets on the cool sand and pulled me into his arms. "Once I came up with this plan, I couldn't get it out of my head the rest of the day." He leaned against me and his thick erection nudged my belly.

I grinned up at him. "Your head? Or some other part?"

"Both." He kissed me as his hands grasped the skirt of my dress. "Because I have a girl who invades every damn minute of my day." He lowered his arms and laid out the blanket. I'd barely sat down and Nix had my dress pushed up to the tops of my thighs. His finger hooked around the top of my panties, and I shifted my bottom as he pulled them down and off my feet.

A cool sea breeze tickled my naked skin. On his hands and knees Nix leaned toward me and kissed me. "Lie back, baby. I want to taste you."

I hesitated and glanced around. We were alone on a beach with just the moonlight for illumination and the ocean for music.

"The seagulls won't tell, and I told them to put away their cameras."

I giggled. "So now you can talk to animals."

"Damn right." His hands pushed open my legs and the gold flecks in his eyes glittered with lust as he gazed down at my pussy. A shivering sensation went through me. I could feel him looking at me, at my most intimate parts, as if he was touching me.

I reclined back on the soft blanket and lifted my hands above my head for a luxurious stretch. Nix took hold of my ankles and slid them toward me so my knees bent. He placed my feet on the blanket. The cool breeze that had tickled my skin felt refreshingly cold on my wet pussy.

Nix lay down on his stomach and began a long, hot trail

of kisses along my inner thighs. The stars overhead blurred as if I could see the movement of the planet. The scenery and fresh air coupled with the feel of Nix's mouth and hands on my naked skin made the moisture between my thighs surge. Nix pushed my thighs open farther, and one hand slipped under my bottom to lift me higher and expose every intimate fold to his probing tongue. It flicked across my clit and I mewled softly into the salty breeze.

Nix always knew exactly what I liked, how much pressure and where to touch to make me crazy with need. His fingers slid through slick moisture and he pressed them deep inside of me. I arched toward his hungry mouth not wanting to miss one stroke of his tongue. I tightened my thighs against his face. I reached down and tangled my fingers in his hair, holding his mouth against me. "God yeah, Nix, Please. More." His fingers moved inside of me finding that spot that nearly made me jump off the blanket. I gripped him with my thighs and ground my pussy and clit against his mouth. "Yes!" I cried out as waves of pure ecstasy rolled through me, tightening my pussy around his hand and tongue. I collapsed against the blanket and reached for him. "Please, Nix, fuck me, please."

With one swift move, he had his shorts pushed down and he was leaning over me. My fingers dug into his arms and I wrapped my legs around his waist as he buried himself in my still aching pussy. My orgasm had not completely subsided, and his cock felt achingly delicious as he thrust hard into me. He reached under my bottom again to lift my hips. He stared down with a heavy-lidded gaze as he rocked against me. "You are all I fucking need, baby. All I need to be happy." His words brought tears to my eyes. I closed them and lifted my bottom higher to take in every thick inch of him. The echoing roar of the waves ricocheted off the cliffs, and the only other sounds were the low groans of pleasure coming from both of us.

"Fuck yeah," Nix muttered, and he lifted higher onto his knees and drove into me with a force that bunched the blanket up beneath us. His fingers dug into my flesh as he came. He relaxed down next to me, and I turned to my side and pressed against him.

He pulled me closer. "You're all I've ever needed, Scotlyn."

All my previous fears and reservations had disappeared. I wanted this man in my life forever. "Nix?"

His breathing was slowing, but I could still feel the beat of his heart against me. "Uh huh?"

I pressed my mouth against his ear. "Marry me."

CHAPTER 20

Nix

The aroma of coffee swirled beneath the door. I got up on my elbow and stared down at Scotlyn. Her smooth skin glowed with a tan and it contrasted with the blonde silky strands of hair framing her face. Her long lashes fluttered open and she smiled at me as she curled her hand behind my neck and pulled me close for a quick kiss.

She stretched. "Is everyone up already?" It was an innocent enough gesture, but it made me instantly hard.

"I know I'm up."

She laughed and reached under the covers. Her fingers grazed my erection. "Oh my, you are wide awake."

Dray's impulsive and highly obnoxious knock rattled the bedroom door. "Hey, you missed the surf. It was awesome. When are you two going to stop playing around and get out here? Cassie and Taylor bought donuts."

Scotlyn popped up on her elbows. "I want the chocolate one with sprinkles," she called.

Dray popped his head in. Scotlyn shrieked and yanked the sheet up over her naked breasts. Dray was unfazed. "Then you better get your butts out here because I'm not risking life and limb to keep donuts away from Clutch."

I threw a pillow at the door and he closed it. "I'm thinking I need my extremely hot fiancé one more time before we hit the pink bakery box. I like the sound of that— extremely hot fiancé. Sounds like something I might order in a fancy restaurant."

"Well, we could just stay engaged forever, then you could keep calling me that. Extremely hot wife doesn't carry that same exotic feel with it."

"On the contrary." I yanked down the sheet and her nipples puckered beneath my gaze. I reached up and teased them between my thumb and forefinger, and she reacted with a deep breath. She arched her back to push them harder against my fingers. "Hmm, I'll be late back from lunch. I'm sneaking home to fuck my extremely hot wife." I kissed her nipple. "I think the phrase works just fine."

She ran her fingers down my chest. "I guess if you put it that way—" Her blue eyes glossed as she gazed up at me. "I'm so happy, Nix."

"Me too, baby." I pulled her naked body beneath me and kissed her.

***

We finally pulled ourselves out of bed and showered and dressed. Dray threw his hands up in the air as we stepped into the small front room. Rett and Finley were out on the patio, and Cassie was on the couch working on her laptop.

"I gave you fair warning," Dray said. "But since you two are acting like teenagers who can't stop groping each other, your choices are pretty damn limited." He lifted a chocolate sprinkled donut out of the box. "However, I did fight Clutch off to save this one for Scottie."

Clutch and Taylor walked in right then. "You didn't fight me off. If I'd wanted the damn donut, it would be in my gut right now, churning around with the other three." He noticed the donut in Scotlyn's hand. "Oh yeah, he did block me from that one. I would have just picked him up and tossed him away from the donut box, but he told me he was saving it for you, Scottie. So I let him think he was a big shot."

Rett and Finley stepped inside. "Hey, guys," Scotlyn said. "What time did you two get in last night?"

"Sometime between you and lover boy's romp down at the beach and your romp in the backseat of his car," Dray answered for them.

I looked over at him with a raised brow. "What the fuck? Were you watching or something?"

Cassie shut her laptop and walked over to me. She put her hand on my shoulder. "Not after I yanked him away from the kitchen window. Just so you know, the street lamp is right over your car. But the windows were fogged enough, leaving an air of mystery around it all."

"It wasn't all that mysterious." Scotlyn shrugged and continued picking the sprinkles off her donut. "We were making out like two groping teens." She winked at Dray. "Two really experienced groping teens."

"Well anyhow, everyone," I spoke up. We'd flipped a coin the night before to see who got to tell everyone, and I'd won. "If you're all done discussing our sex life, I have an announcement to make."

141

Cassie and Taylor squealed simultaneously. I looked over at them. "I haven't even said anything yet."

They squealed again and ran over to Scotlyn, who managed to hang on to her donut as they hugged her. Scotlyn opened her arm so Finley could join in. They took a quick breather to check out the ring. It was a solitary diamond with a platinum band. I knew Scotlyn liked simple and elegant, and she seemed to love it.

"Damn, I guess I don't have to announce anything," I said disappointedly.

Cassie pulled away from the group hug long enough to roll her eyes at me. "Please, Scottie texted Taylor and me last night."

"When?" Scotlyn and I had barely parted long enough to take a breath, let alone text friends.

"Just before the backseat romp," Scotlyn said.

The girls finally let each other go. "I'll bring my laptop down to the beach, and we can start plans," Cassie said.

"Wait, don't you want to know when?" I asked, and then felt instantly stupid when Cassie rolled her eyes again.

"End of August," Cassie said as if she was giving me the information. "Which gives us only six weeks."

I looked at Scotlyn. "Shit, how many texts were you sending while I thought you were, you know, in the throes of passion?"

Now she blushed. "Just a few important ones."

Taylor hopped up and down. "I am so going to get an A on that dress now. I'll even have real wedding pictures." She stopped hopping and fell uncharacteristically quiet. "Unless you want to buy another dress. I'd understand,

Scottie."

Scotlyn hugged her again. "Are you kidding? I think trying on that dress yesterday sort of prodded me into action. It was so perfect and so lovely. It made me feel like a bride."

My buddies stood around this whole scene with expressions of shock and dismay carved into their stony faces.

"Prodded *you* into action?" Clutch finally asked.

Scotlyn glanced my way.

"Doesn't bother me," I told her. "You're obviously better at it than me."

"I'm the one who proposed this time," Scotlyn said.

Dray's eyes bulged. "Holy shit, Nix, what have you done? You're just opening us all up for trouble with that."

I walked over and slapped his shoulder harder than I needed to, but I knew he had a nice sunburn. His reaction assured me it was still bad. "That's right, best man." I knew the words would catch Clutch's attention, but Scottie and I had discussed the whole problem of me having two best friends.

She walked over to Clutch, took hold of his hands and peered up at him. I could see her eyes were already wet with tears before she even spoke. She smiled, and immediately, it worked its magic on his frown. "Clutch, would you please do me the honor of walking me down the aisle?"

He shot a tough shit look at Dray, then returned his attention to Scotlyn. "The honor would be mine."

CHAPTER 21

Scotlyn

Finley dropped her phone into her lap and stretched out her suntanned legs over the sand. "It's settled. The wedding will take place at the King estate." She lifted up her finger. "But, my dad has one stipulation. He wants to sing at the wedding."

"Oh my god. Nicky King singing at our wedding would be surreal." We'd pulled our chairs into a huddle on the beach and stuck the 'girls only' ice chest in the center for refreshments and to act as an impromptu desk for Cassie's laptop. The guys had quickly bored of wedding plans and headed back into the water.

Cassie and Finley together were like a pair of supercharged dynamos. Taylor and I had a hard time keeping up with the ideas that they volleyed back and forth. Nix had warned me that Cassie would probably get a little crazy with involvement, but I was thankful. I had absolutely no idea what went into planning a wedding. But I'd made her promise to keep it small and low-key. Of course, adding Nicky King, the lead singer of Black Thunder, to the music list might just have taken low-key off the table completely.

"So, is it all right if my dad sings at the wedding?"

"Are you kidding, Finley?" I asked. "Nix just might pass out when I tell him. Please be sure to thank him for letting us use his place, and tell him that having him sing will be something that I'll never forget."

"I'll just have to make sure he doesn't get too drunk, otherwise his song lyrics become one long smear of British slang."

"Really?" Taylor asked.

"Yeah, when he's too drunk, he forgets the words and sticks in the phrase 'bloody hell' to fill in any gaps."

Taylor laughed. "O.K., now we have to make sure he drinks too much." She stared down at the sketchpad she'd carried out to the sand. "Scottie, have you decided on a color to add?"

I relaxed back. "I have. My mom's favorite color was hot pink. I think we could use a softer, more twenty-first century, shade of hot pink. What do you think?"

She tapped her pencil against her chin. "Yes, pink will work." She lifted the sketchpad up and showed us her drawings for the bridesmaid dresses. They were beautiful, mid-thigh length with petticoats sticking out from the skirt and a halter style top.

Finley leaned forward. "That is gorgeous. You and Cassie will look adorable in that style."

I looked over at her. "What about you, Finley? Would you please be a bridesmaid? I know Nix is planning to ask Rett."

Finley flipped her sunglasses up on her head. "Really? I would love it. Are you sure?"

"To be honest, Finley, I just assumed you were going to

be up there with me."

She reached across and our chairs nearly toppled together as we hugged.

Cassie harrumphed. "We've got a problem. Nix's two nephews can be in the wedding party, but what about flower girls? I don't know any little girls." She looked at Taylor, who shook her head.

Finley picked up her phone. "I know two of the absolutely cutest little girls on the planet."

"Finley, I don't know if Some Pig can carry a basket of rose petals."

"No he can't" Finley laughed. "And he would eat the rose petals before they fluttered to the ground. Besides, Some Pig is a boy." Finley tapped her head. "Which reminds me, I need to make a mental note to remember to have a tuxedo made for Some Pig. He'll be really pissed if he doesn't have something to wear to the wedding." She looked over at me. "Will it be all right if he comes?"

"Of course. I'd be hurt if Some Pig didn't attend."

Finley started dialing her phone. "Anyhow, back to the flower girls." Someone answered. "Hey, Eden, do you think Sophie and Janie would like to be flower girls in a wedding? No, Rett didn't propose. Nix and Scotlyn are getting married at our house at the end of August. Scottie's right here." She paused and pressed the button for speakerphone.

"Congratulations, Scotlyn. You two are so perfect together."

"Thank you, Eden."

"And as far as my sisters wanting to be flower girls— let me just say, those two breathe, eat and sleep princesshood.

Hand them two frilly dresses and baskets of rose petals and they will be the two happiest girls on Earth."

"Great," I said. "Thanks so much. We'll get the dresses if you can just get us their sizes."

"You bet, and congrats. I'm excited for you."

Finley put the phone back to her ear. "Thanks, Eden. I'll let you break the news to your sisters. Bye." She hung up. "Man, we should all start a business called Insta-wedding. Scotlyn, you'll still have to pick a cake and flowers."

I looked out to the water. Nix and Dray were laughing about something. "You guys, thanks. This all means so much to me." Not having my mom and sister around had cast a shadow over any thoughts of marriage, but my friends had stepped in to fill the void. I thought about how rough things were just a few weeks ago and the despair I'd been feeling, but at the moment, I was having a hard time keeping myself from floating up off the beach chair.

Chapter 22

Scotlyn

Two weeks into the wedding planning and I wondered when and why we'd dropped elopement off the table. But I was lucky. Cassie loved this kind of stuff, and she'd stepped in to do most of it. All I had to do was make some superficial decisions, and she handled everything else.

We'd kept the budget pretty small. Both Nix and I had agreed that we didn't want to pour a lot of money into it. We just wanted to make sure our friends had a good time. And it was mostly friends. Once we got back from the beach trip, we'd sat down to make a list for invites, which Cassie had insisted needed to go out right away. Nix and I had a good, long laugh at how pathetic the list was on the family end. I, of course, had no one, which I'd known all along, but it looked especially sad when I saw it on paper. My aunt, my only one living relative, was not going to be invited. Nix would, of course, send an invite to his mom, but he was sure she wouldn't come. Nix's friends were my friends too now, which made sharing spots on the list much easier. I had some friends in nursing school, but they were about the only people on the list who hadn't actually come from Nix's side. It was as if the accident had severed all my ties with the world. And in truth, it had.

Clutch had given me the rest of the afternoon off to check out florists. I'd visited five shops and had received the same look of shock from all of them. The wedding was too close. Each of the florists had scoffed and told me there was no way. But I remembered a new, little flower shop had opened just blocks from Freefall, and it seemed to be having trouble competing with some of the bigger stores in town. I parked the car in one of the three spaces out front of the shop.

It had taken me a good week to get back behind the wheel of a car. Nix had been thoroughly patient with me as if he was teaching me to drive all over again. And that's almost how it felt. Getting *back on the horse* as they say isn't all that easy when you've taken a really bad fall. But it was nearly impossible to live in California without a car. Finley, whose trouble with anxiety had made driving a challenge as well, taught me several more breathing techniques. And they worked surprisingly well.

The shop was called Flower Power, and the whole place reminded me of my bohemian parents. A young girl came out from behind a long curtain of beads. She was wearing a suede vest with long fringes and a thin headband of small roses.

"How can I help you?" she asked.

"I'm getting married in four weeks, and I need a florist. I know it's short notice."

She pulled out a catalog and a pad of paper. I hadn't noticed her giant smile until she pulled up a stool. "I'll do it."

"You will? Oh, thank you." She pointed to another stool, and I sat down. "You know, my dress designer has been trying to decide on a headpiece to go with the dress. Do you think you could make me a headband of small pink and red roses? Or is that too much to ask at such short notice?"

She wrote it down. "I can make you an absolutely gorgeous one. Not that you'll need much help in the beautiful bride department, but red and pink will look stunning in your blonde hair."

I reached over and patted her hand. "Thank you for taking this on at such short notice."

She glanced around at her sadly empty shop. Her arrangements were uniquely beautiful and all she needed was some exposure. "No, thank you. I'm afraid the reality of breaking into this business has hit me hard. I can't wait to do this. Where will the wedding take place?"

"In Beverly Hills at the Nicky King estate."

She nearly slipped off the stool. "You're marrying Nicky King? No wonder you're so gorgeous."

"No, his daughter is a friend of mine. He will be singing at my wedding. Tell you what, make an extra nice boutonniere for him, and I'll see that my photographer gets a picture of him wearing it. He's a super nice man. I'm sure he'll let you put the picture in your wedding catalog."

Her smile brightened more. "Let's get started."

***

Nix's car wasn't in front of Freefall. Cassie had taken him to get fitted for a tux, but I was sure they would have been back already. Our cake tasting session had been moved up half an hour. It was the only thing that Nix had wanted to be involved in, only because it meant trying a variety of cakes and frostings. I decided to go inside and wait for him. It had been months since I'd had time to visit Freefall.

Cassie had rearranged some of the furniture, and there were new art samples up on the wall. Otherwise, it was the same shop where I'd met and fallen in love with the owner. The first time I'd stepped inside the place, I hadn't wanted to be there at all. But Lincoln, the man who had saved me from the streets only to make me his possession, had insisted that the owner was considered the best in town. Lincoln couldn't stand the long jagged scar on my side, left behind by the windshield of my dad's car. He'd had an artist design a long, trailing vine of pink flowers to cover it. It was during those intimate tattoo sessions that I'd fallen in love with Nix. I was unable to talk, but he listened to every word I had to say, whether through gestures or print. Lincoln had sensed something between us. Anyone could have seen it. The heat between Nix and me had been palpable. Lincoln had decided to switch artists, but I'd put my foot down, something I'd rarely done, mostly because after losing my family nothing else ever mattered enough for me to bother. But Nix had mattered. He had been the first thing that mattered after my life had been shattered on that mountainside.

A girl with red hair and a tiny skirt and halter top came out from the back. She was pretty, but there was nothing inviting about her smile. "Stormy, right?"

"Yep, that's me."

"I'm Scotlyn," I stuck out my hand. She took it, but still acted as if she had no idea who I was. I knew that Nix had my picture on his desk. It was obvious she was going to play dumb. "I'm Nix's girl— fiancé."

"Oh, right," she said, sounding bored with our brief conversation. "Congrats on that."

I'd planned to wait around for Nix, but Stormy wasn't making that idea seem to palatable. I reached over to Cassie's sticky note pad and grabbed a pen. "I'm going to leave this note for Nix. If you could see that he gets it." I scribbled down that cake tasting had been moved up half an hour and to meet me at the bakery. I would get there early and treat myself to a brownie. With the flower order behind me, I was feeling like I needed a reward.

I handed her the note.

"Okie dokie," she said tersely.

I walked out. It'd definitely been her perfume I'd smelled on Nix's sweatshirt.

CHAPTER 23

Nix

Cassie had gone home early. She'd been doing double duty working at Freefall and being the wedding planner of the century. I finished arranging the next week's schedule and had just enough time to get to the bakery to taste cake. My phone buzzed.

"Hey, baby, I'm just leaving the shop."

"Didn't you get my note?" Scotlyn sounded confused. "They moved the tasting up half an hour. I just finished."

"What note?"

"I wrote it on a pink sticky note and told Stormy to give it to you."

Stormy was cleaning up tools in the back room. I glanced around the counter. "I don't see it. Stormy was with a client when I got back from the tux fitting. She might have forgotten. I'm sorry about that. I'm bummed I missed tasting all that cake. Did you make a decision?"

"Yep. Marble. That way chocolate lovers and white cake lovers will be satisfied. And now I'm feeling like slipping into a sugar coma."

"Damn, I should have been there. I love cake." As I

walked past the end of the counter something pink caught my eye in the trash can. Scotlyn said something else but I missed it. I leaned down and grabbed the pink sticky note with Scotlyn's message out of the trash. "Shit."

"What's the matter?" Scotlyn asked.

"Oh, nothing, but I've got to go. Hey, I'm closing up in an hour. Why don't you come back to the shop, and we can go get something to eat."

"Doubt I'll be able to eat anything after all that cake, but I'll be there. I'm about forty minutes away with traffic."

"See you then."

I walked into the back with the pink note stuck to my palm. Stormy was washing up. She turned around for a second and then returned to her work.

"I guess Scotlyn came in to leave me a message, huh?"

Her eyes were wide as she turned back around. She smacked the side of her head with her palm. "Oh, that's right. Your cake tasting has been moved up." She spun back around to the sink.

"I guess my next question would be why the hell did you drop the note in the trash?"

She shrugged but kept wiping off her equipment. "Did I? Must have been an accident. Sorry."

I scrubbed my hair with my fingers, a gesture due to a mix of frustration and disappointment. "Yeah, me too."

She was either clueless about my anger or purposely ignoring it.

I walked over to her. "Look, you're an extremely talented artist, Stormy, and some other shop will be glad to have you. But you're done at Freefall."

She paused for a second and twisted her lips angrily. "Seriously? I throw away one note, and you're fucking firing me?"

"Yeah, I am. But it's not just the note, and you know it."

She started piling up her tools. "Whatever. But you'll be losing customers."

"Chance I'll have to take. I'll go figure out what I owe you and write you a check."

It didn't take Stormy long to gather her stuff. I was bummed. She really did great work, but there was something about her that wasn't sitting right. I was relieved when she huffed out the door with her bag. Scotlyn walked in just a few minutes later.

She leaned over to look through to the back room. "Stormy is off for the day?"

"For forever. I let her go. I found your pink note in the trash."

"Oh." She looked a little perplexed. "Maybe it fell in there. Although, I have to say her manner at the counter when I walked in earlier was a little off-putting."

"Yeah, she did off-putting really well. I'll find someone else." I reached for her hand and pulled her into my arms. "Hmm, you smell like buttercream frosting."

She pressed her hand to her stomach. "Oh my gosh, don't even bring up frosting. You know I consider myself the queen of the sweet tooths, but that was too much cake even for me."

"You poor baby, I sent you to do that treacherous work all by yourself." My hand swept beneath the hem of her shirt. I smoothed my palm along her back. "I wonder if I can still taste our wedding cake choice on your lips." I lowered my face and kissed her. Her hands wrapped around my neck and her lips parted for my kiss to go deeper.

I lifted my mouth from hers. "You know, I am done for today. I just need to put a few things in the autoclave. Why don't you come into my laboratory, my sweet cake taster?"

"Only if you promise to keep kissing me like you are now," she said.

"Among other things." I walked to the door, turned over the sign and locked up the shop. I spun around. "It is good to be boss." I took her hand and led her into the tattoo room. She hoisted herself up on the table. It was propped up in the back, but the leg piece was down.

"You know, I've been thinking," she said. "I would like to have my lover's name tattooed on my body. I know I don't have an appointment, but I've heard you're the best in town."

I pulled up my chair and sat in front of her. I trailed my hands along the skin of her legs. "Your lover? Lucky man. And exactly where would you like this tattoo?"

She tapped her lush bottom lip, and I wanted to draw that lip in between my teeth. She parted her legs and moved her fingers along the creamy white skin of her inner thigh stopping just an inch from the top. "Right here. Can you do it?"

The thought of tattooing my name just a hair's breadth from her sweet pussy made me hard. I peered up at her. She was the perfect mix of innocent and sultry, and, as always, she made me nuts with wanting her.

"You'll have to be willing to strip down," I said.

"If I must."

"I'll get my tools, you get naked. And I mean completely naked." I walked to the counter and flipped on the radio. Scotlyn jumped down from the table and slid off her sandals. I busied myself for a few seconds with the ink but couldn't keep my mind on my task. The next time I glanced back, Scotlyn had removed her shirt and shorts. I couldn't stop myself. I was in front of her in two long steps. I slid her bra straps down over her shoulders, exposing her breasts. I yanked her panties down to the floor, and she stepped out of them.

She stepped forward, and I held her naked body against me.

"I remember when I first sat in this room with you." She gazed up at me with her blue eyes. "My life changed that day. For the first time since my accident, I badly wanted to talk. There was something so compelling about the way you looked at me." She reached up and put her palm against my face. "I wanted to tell you everything about me. I wanted every emotion that I'd been holding in just to spill out onto this tile floor. You were basically a stranger, but you listened to me with your heart." She pressed her hand against my chest. "I couldn't believe how quickly I became attached to you." She smiled but tears came with it. "I remember the first time I heard my voice again was when you touched me. We were on the houseboat, and you touched me. I wanted you so badly, a sound rolled out of my throat."

I caressed her silky skin. "I remember. It was just a small, soft sound. Trust me, I've never been so turned on by anything in my life." I dropped my arms. "I've got something to show you." I walked over to the cabinet where I kept my drawings and artwork. I reached in and pulled out the pieces of paper I'd kept tucked inside.

Scotlyn glanced at them, confused at first but then she recognized the papers. I handed them to her, and she shuffled through them and laughed. "Break. Ouch. Ouch!! All good." Her eyes were shiny as she smiled up at me. "The notes I used during the tattoo to let you know how I was feeling. You kept them."

"Yep. Just in case you thought I wasn't sentimental."

She hopped up on her tiptoes and kissed me. "Well, you did keep my picture in your wallet long before you met me." She placed the notes on my work counter and strolled over to the table.

She lifted herself up onto it and leaned back on her hands. "Sitting here on this table, while you drew that tattoo on me, was the most erotic experience ever. And today, we don't have to worry about anyone barging in or keeping an eye on me because I am yours, and yours only."

I walked over and grabbed her into my arms. My mouth slammed down over hers. She reached for the fly on my jeans and opened it. A groan rumbled in my throat as she pushed down my pants and took hold of my cock. It strained against her fingers as she twirled her thumb around the moist tip. I lifted her hand away, not having enough will to withstand her teasing. I took both her slim wrists in one hand and held her arms above her head as she leaned against the backrest. I held her captive as I dragged her bottom closer to the edge of the table and pushed her thighs open wider with my free hand.

She gazed at me from beneath heavy dark lashes, her

eyes taking on an unearthly sapphire blue, as she watched me enter her. I dropped my gaze down to my cock and watched it slide into her tight, wet pussy. Her head lulled back and her lips parted as she moaned in pleasure.

I held tightly to her hands as she arched her back in an effort to take in more of me. "God, Nix, I'm already close." She tried to tug her hands free but I held her, wanting to be able to watch her entire body as she came.

"You are a masterpiece, baby, a fucking work of art." I shoved my cock deeper, and she clenched her legs around my waist to draw me in farther. She ground the slick folds of her pussy against me.

"Don't stop," she whimpered. "Don't ever stop."

"Never."

A pink blush covered her face and shoulders, and her nipples puckered into small rose-colored buds. Her pussy tightened around my cock in shuddering waves.

I released her hands and took hold of her hips, yanking her even closer as I pushed inside. She was tight and hot around me as I slammed into her. She lifted her heavy head. Her eyes opened slowly, and now, like I'd watched her, she gazed at me with eyes still glassy from ecstasy. I moved inside of her, bringing myself to the edge and over it. I leaned down my hands on either side of her legs to catch my breath.

Scotlyn reached up and took hold of my face to kiss it. "Now about that tattoo?"

A laugh shot out of my mouth. "You might have to give me a second here." I dragged my fingers down her breast. "To be honest, this might be the most difficult tattoo I've ever done."

"Just three letters?"

"Yes, and with my face and hands tucked between your legs. By the way, you'll be a little sore there for a few days. Are you sure about it?"

She leaned forward and placed her arms around my neck. "Having your name in a spot where only you can see it— I want it. Please."

I kissed her. "I'll get my stuff together."

"Should I get at least partially dressed?"

"What kind of a mad man would I have to be to say yes to that?" I walked over to my work counter.

She hopped off the table, and I was disappointed to see her pick up her shorts.

"What are you doing?" I asked. "Change your mind?"

She pulled a folded paper from her pocket. "Nope, but I wanted to show you something." I turned and leaned against the counter. She forced back a grin as she unfolded the paper and smiled up at me.

"Once Nana had finished reciting her memoirs to me, I typed them into the computer and had the manuscript printed. I sent it off to some publishers without Nana knowing. I was hoping I could surprise her with it, but unfortunately..." Her words fell off. She cleared her throat and read from the letter. "Dear Ms. James, Our editorial team has reviewed your manuscript titled Life's a Peach, and we are excited to let you know that we would like to publish the book."

"Holy shit, Nana's memoirs? God, Scotlyn, you never stop amazing me. She would be so damn excited. Hell, I'm so damn excited. I'll have to call Diana later." I took her into my arms. "But for now, I'm about to do the best damn tattoo of my career."

Chapter 24

Scotlyn

"All three bridesmaid dresses have been cut, and I started sewing bodices." Taylor stepped forward in the line. The band was just getting started. Dray and Cassie were already inside, hopefully snagging us a table. I'd told Cassie I didn't want any bridal shower because there wasn't enough time to make people attend both that and a wedding a few weeks later. And I really didn't need anything. Nix and I had everything we could want. So we'd decided a night out with just the four couples would be a way to make up for it. Finley and Rett had been too busy with the barn, so it was just the six of us.

"I can't wait to see the dresses, Taylor. And I will pay you for all your time, even if you won't let me pay you for material."

She waved off the suggestion as she always did. "I told you, this is such a valuable opportunity for me that I need no payment. Besides, I travel to the garment district downtown once a week. The fabrics are high quality and dirt cheap."

The club allowed eighteen-year-olds and up, but anyone under twenty-one was branded with a black X on the back of their hand to keep them from buying alcohol. Taylor was still more than a year away from being able to drink legally, and it always produced a pout. But tonight, she took her black hand stamp with a smile, and we walked into the club.

Cassie waved us over. It seemed they'd grabbed the best table in the place. It was just ten steps from the bar but a much farther distance from the speakers. We pushed through the crowded bar area to the table. Cassie leaned closer so she wouldn't have to shout over the noise. "I ordered some margaritas."

We pulled out chairs and sat. Nix and Dray set off toward the bar. Clutch and Taylor were across from me. There seemed to be some tension between them but then that was usual. Taylor, who looked especially beautiful with her copper penny hair swept up in a ponytail, reached into her purse, glanced around and quickly untwisted the top from a small flask. She lifted it to her mouth, took a short swig and then replaced the top. She dropped it back into her purse and met Clutch's eyes as she looked up.

"What?" she asked with complete innocence. "I bought it at the mall." She lifted her purse and opened it but didn't remove the flask again. "Isn't it cute? It has tiny pink skulls on it."

"Let me see it." Clutch held out his palm. She peeked around before handing it to him. He folded his fingers around it and got up. Taylor's eyes opened wide as she watched him lumber across the room and toss the flask into a trash can. I glanced over at Cassie, who pulled her lips tight and gave a tiny shrug.

Taylor crossed her arms and slumped down in her chair.

One moment she was a woman and the next a teenager. I tried to remember if I'd ever straddled that line, but life on the streets had wiped away my teen attitude pretty quickly.

I leaned across the table. "Taylor, if you were caught, they'd kick you right out of here. They might even call the cops. These places have to be extremely careful about minors and alcohol, or they get shut down."

Her green eyes were wet with tears, and it seemed she wasn't going to come out of her sulk anytime soon. The guys returned to the table with their beers. Clutch placed a coke down in front of Taylor. She pushed it away, but for a second, I was certain she would dump it in his lap.

In typical guy fashion, Nix and Dray had not clued in to the tension at the table. "Rett said Nicky King has invited us to come to the house early for the wedding, a little luxury vacation at our best friend's, the mega-rock star, estate." Dray looked eagerly around the table. His confused glance landed on Clutch, whose expression bordered on icy. No one answered, but it seemed that Nix had finally noticed a problem.

"Shit, why is everyone so grumpy?" Dray asked.

Cassie slid off her chair. "Shut up and let's dance. You can put that fancy fighter's footwork to good use."

Dray got up and followed Cassie to the floor.

"You could have at least let me put it back in my purse," Taylor said suddenly.

Clutch drank some beer but didn't look at her.

She thumped him on the arm, which was pretty meaningless on an arm his size, but some of his beer splashed from the glass.

167

"When are you going to stop treating me like a kid?" she asked.

Clutch stared down at her but didn't need to answer. I badly wanted to help Taylor, but shedding the teen years was something she was going to have to figure out on her own. She'd set her sights on a man six years older, and sometimes the age difference was quite noticeable. And, on top of that, Clutch tended to be an older and more mature twenty-five than most.

Taylor obviously decided that slumping down on a chair next to her enormous boyfriend wasn't working in her favor. She straightened and thrust her chin defiantly forward. Nix and I pretended to busy ourselves with our drinks and with people watching.

"You're an arrogant asshole, and I'd have more fun going out with my father than you," Taylor said sharply.

"Then I'll take you home and you two can make plans."

Nix got up and lowered his hand for me to take. "They're playing our song."

"I didn't know we had a song." I placed my hand on his.

"We do now."

It wasn't a slow song but Nix pulled me against him and we shuffled our feet over the wood floor. We stayed on the outer edge of the dance floor. Dray and Cassie were tearing it up in the middle.

I laughed. "He really is light on his feet."

"Yep, that's one of the reasons he's so damn good in the octagon. That, and his supernatural ability to not feel any pain." Nix glanced back to the table. "What did I miss? They didn't walk in that pissed at each other."

"Taylor brought in a flask with alcohol, and Clutch threw it away."

Nix laughed. "That explains things. I'm kind of worried about those two. If Taylor doesn't mature a little more and a little faster, Clutch might not stick around."

"But he's crazy about her. And he needs to cut her a little slack. She's nineteen. She's getting more mature all the time. I can tell you, she has an amazing talent that will take her far. It will be Clutch's loss if he can't show a little more tolerance." I hadn't meant to sharpen my tone, but the more I thought about it, the more I decided that Clutch was being too hard. "The last thing Taylor needs is another controlling parent in her life."

Nix leaned back. "Hey, why am I getting the tongue lashing?"

"Sorry, my frustration was aimed at Clutch. Not you." I lowered my head onto his shoulder. "I guess the next time we dance, we'll be husband and wife."

"Yes, and Nicky King will be singing. How fucking cool is that?"

I smiled. "Not exactly where I thought my last sentiment would lead, but yeah, it's amazing."

"Oh, and as Nicky sings, I will be holding the most incredible woman in the world, in my arms."

"That's better." We twirled around, and I now had a view of our table. Taylor had gotten up. She was propped up on a barstool talking animatedly with two guys. Clutch sat with stiff shoulders, and his fingers wrapped tightly around his beer, trying his damndest not to look Taylor's direction. Not thinking, I brought up the subject of Clutch and Taylor again. "Still, I can see Taylor's point of view. I've lived with a controlling man, who told me what to wear and how to behave, and it's not fun."

Nix dropped his arms and stepped back. His face was hard. "You've got to stop comparing every guy to that prick you used to live with." He marched off the floor and left me standing alone, wondering how I'd managed to get my foot all the way up to my mouth.

I walked back to the table and sat down. Dray and Cassie came off the floor too. It was not exactly the fun and laughter filled night we'd anticipated. I motioned secretly toward Taylor, and Cassie glanced her direction. Her shoulders sank. The mood around the table was grim. Then, Clutch's chair scraped the ground, and he pounded across the floor toward Taylor. She looked up with fake alarm. Again, she knew exactly what she was doing. Unlike the body surfers at the beach, these two guys didn't seem as inclined to back down from the giant heading toward them.

Dray looked at Nix. "This should go well."

Clutch stopped in front of Taylor, completely ignoring the two knuckleheads who seemed to have delusions of immortality. He said something and then stormed out the exit door. Taylor's face went pale, and she looked ready to pass out. Cassie and I shot out of our chairs and raced over to her.

She dropped right into my arms. "Clutch just broke up with me." She was in full sobbing mode by the time we got her to the table. We sat her down and pulled up chairs on each side of her.

"Shouldn't you two go after Clutch?" I asked.

"What for?" Nix responded.

170

I sighed loudly in frustration, and Cassie shook her head at them.

"Look," Dray said, and I knew something obnoxious would follow. "When we guys are pissed, we don't sit down with buckets of ice cream and soothe and coddle and analyze what went wrong."

"No," Cassie erupted, "you grunt and toss around the word 'fuck' a dozen times and in every form of speech and then you snort down enough beer to put a foamy head on your piss."

Dray lifted a finger. "And don't forget wall punching. Punching holes in a wall is an extremely important part of the man tantrum. Clutch is probably outside right now blowing a Viking-sized hole through the wall of this building."

Taylor shook with sobs. I handed her a napkin, but it wasn't enough to sop up the river of tears. She looked across the table. "Nix, please," she cried, "go talk to him. Tell him I didn't mean it."

Nix looked at me first and then at Taylor. "Sorry, sweetie, this is something you started. You're going to have to make it right."

Taylor collapsed against me. Our table was garnering a lot of attention now. Cassie pulled her keys out of her purse. "Scottie and I are going to take Taylor to our house for awhile." She threw the keys at Dray. "Now, your plan to get, as you'd so eloquently put it, shitfaced has been thwarted. You've just become the designated driver."

I put my arm around Taylor's shoulder, and we walked her out of the bar.

171

Cassie didn't have any buckets of ice cream, but we did manage to polish off a bag of M&Ms. Or at least Cassie and I did. Taylor was in no mood to eat. She was still sniffling up a storm as I dropped her off at her house. Cassie and I had tried to gently let her know that she had to stop teasing Clutch by flirting with other guys. She seemed to mull that notion over some between insisting she didn't need the guy and exclaiming that she couldn't live without him.

I knew them both well enough to know that they weren't over. They'd just hit a rough patch like the one that Nix and I had just hiked through. And tonight hadn't been all, as Nana would say, sugar and roses between us. There were times when we went out as couples that everything felt right and balanced. Then there were other times, like tonight, when the stark difference between men and women burned so brightly, it disrupted that harmony.

The kitchen light was on as I pulled into the driveway. Ironically enough, Nix was at the table, leaning over a carton of ice cream, digging into it with a soup spoon. He looked up and I pointed to my own mouth to let him know about the ice cream on his lip. He wiped it away and dropped the spoon in the carton.

He leaned back and held his arms out. "What the hell just happened? I thought we were going out for a few beers and some dancing. How'd it go so wrong?"

"It seems you followed through on the few beers." I pulled up a chair and dragged the ice cream carton in front of me. "Taylor was obviously too upset to stay out, and Cassie and I are her closest friends. Did you ever talk to

Clutch?"

He shook his head. "Nope. I'm sure he just needs to cool off. He loves Taylor. She just needs to grow up."

I looked over at him. "He knew she was six years younger. He needs to keep that in mind. She'll mature soon enough, and frankly, some of her best personality traits come from her being a wild teenager. Sometimes, I wish I had some of her spunk." I picked up the spoon and dug into the ice cream. "All the peanut butter chunks are gone."

"Yep, because I went through and picked out each one."

"You pig." I had Nix's full attention as I slid the spoonful of ice cream into my mouth. "You know," I said, "that tattoo is all healed up. But, I think, just in case, my tattoo artist should check it out."

His chair tipped back on two legs as he got up. He lowered his hand to mine. "I'm at your service, milady." He had definitely had more than his share of beer.

I stood up and before I could protest, he swept me up into his arms and carried me through the family room to the hallway, nearly crowning my head on the doorway as he glided through it.

I peered up at him. "I think this is supposed to be after the wedding and over the threshold."

"Should I put you down?" His breath was rich with the smell of beer.

I wrapped my arms around his neck. "Nope, just mentioning." We got to the bedroom door, and he whipped my feet around to push the door open.

"I am now carrying my extremely hot fiancé, soon to be extremely hot wife, to the bed for sex."

I laughed. "Are you really going to narrate this because it's kind of a mood killer."

"Then I'll shut up." He dropped me onto the bed. "But one day, I'm going to narrate the whole thing. I think it would be fucking cool. She swoons as I rip the panties off of her." He looked down for affirmation, but I laughed in response. "It would be like reading one of Cassie's novels aloud."

"All right, my more than slightly drunk husband to be, grasp that great, glistening, throbbing manhood from your breeches otherwise this hot, wet sheath is going out to watch television."

He unzipped his pants and then something seemed to have struck him. "Manhood? Really? Is that what word they use?"

"Sometimes."

"Manhood. Hmm, manhood," he repeated in a deeper voice. "I like it. I might just have it tattooed on the side of my—"

I wrapped my and around his neck and pulled his mouth down over mine.

CHAPTER 25

Nix

"Oh my gosh, Nix, you have to come see this article about Finley's rescue barn," Cassie called from the front of the shop.

I was readying the ink for my next tattoo. "Is that the one with the pictures you took?"

"No, this one is different."

"What's it say?" I was still yelling, but she'd already snuck in behind me. I turned around and startled. "Shit, you must have tiptoed. So what's in it?"

"It talks about Finley's barn and the great work she is doing with Barrett Mason, her partner."

I set up a line of tiny paper cups. "That's cool."

"That's not the part I wanted you to see." She lifted the paper to read. "Some of our readers might be wondering just what Finley King's famous father has been up to since he took a break from concert tours. Finley assures us that Nicky King is enjoying his time off, but he's still performing. This summer he will sing at a wedding for two of Finley's friends, Nix Pierce, son of the late race car driver, Alexander Pierce and Scotlyn James. The wedding will take place at the King estate."

I grabbed the paper. "Hey, we got a wedding announcement in the paper just like important, famous people."

"Ooh, that reminds me. I need to check on Taylor and the dresses. After the little fiasco the other night, I'm worried she's not going to get the dresses finished." Cassie walked out still talking.

My phone rang. I hadn't talked to Clutch since he'd walked out of the bar. He wasn't the type to pry, and he was definitely not the type to want to share either. "Hey, Clutch, what's up?"

"Car meet Friday at seven." He sounded down.

"All right. Scottie and I don't have anything else going on. You doing all right?"

"Fucking grand. Christ, just don't know if this relationship thing is worth the hassle, you know?" Apparently today, he was in a rare sharing mood. "I mean, I'm constantly having to worry about saying the right thing or buying the right gift or satisfying her when—well, you know, but she just does whatever the fuck she wants. And she expects me to be all right with it."

"Uh, isn't this a conversation you should be having with Taylor?"

He sighed loudly. "Yeah, I just don't feel like talking to her right now."

"You should wait then, but I'd tell her everything you just told me."

"It's easier saying it to you because—"

"Because I don't make you horny by just breathing softly into the phone?"

176

"Yeah, something like that. Plus, she doesn't let me finish before she starts spurting tears and stomping off."

"That can be a problem. Those tears are dangerous damn weapons."

"Yep, that they are. Well, I'll be out there at seven on Friday. See you then."

"Later."

I walked to the front of the shop. Cassie didn't seem to be having a great phone conversation either. "I know, Taylor, except the wedding is just a few weeks away, and we can't send the bride down the aisle in shorts and sandals."

"I'd still marry her," I interrupted.

Cassie waved for me to shut up, so I returned to my ink.

CHAPTER 26

Scotlyn

Things had been going well with wedding plans, which, of course, meant it was high times things went awry. From what I'd read, there was no such thing as completely smooth sailing when it came to weddings, and that would be especially true for ones that were planned only a month and a half out from the engagement.

Taylor was a mess, and it seemed that the dresses might not get done in time. I told Cassie not to stress about it, but she seemed to stress more over the fact that I wasn't stressed about it.

The phone rang as soon as I stepped out of the car. It was Cassie. Lately, she was skipping the greeting and getting right to the meat of the conversation. "Did Nix show you the article in the paper about Finley's barn and your wedding announcement?"

"Yes, it's sitting inside, on our kitchen table. Pretty cool."

"I was thinking, maybe if we went over to Taylor's and offered to help in some way."

"I don't know about you, but I'm no help at all when

it comes to sewing." I leaned down and picked up a small cube shaped box that the mailman had left on the porch. It was addressed to Ms. Scotlyn James. The return address was from someone named Parker who lived in Burbank. I knew no one with that name or anyone who lived in Burbank, for that matter.

"I can't sew a button on without stabbing ten holes in my finger, but maybe we could cut fabric or something," Cassie continued. "We just need to get her mind off Clutch and back on the dresses."

Nix's car drove up just as I stepped inside the house.

"I don't know what to say, Cassie. We can always just buy some dresses off the rack if she doesn't finish in time."

"Off the rack? That would suck. And I still haven't found anyone to do lighting on such short notice. We might be walking around in our leftover prom dresses holding flashlights in our bouquets. The flowers are still happening, right?"

"As far as I know. The girl was pretty new to the business but happy to do it. I guess we'll see if she delivers."

Cassie grunted. "Clutch is having problems finding a tuxedo to fit him. Apparently tuxes don't come in Viking sizes. But, on the bright side, Dray tried one on and thought he looked so damn good, he wants to have one made out of spandex. Thinks he can be the only tux wearing fighter on the circuit. Just not sure what to do about Clutch."

"Maybe we could shrink him," I suggested, but Cassie just wasn't in the mood for humor. "We planned to marry at the end of August because I start back at school in September, but now I'm wondering if we should have just eloped."

Cassie was silent. My thoughtless words had hurt her. She'd been working so hard on this wedding and I'd callously suggested running off to elope.

"No, I didn't mean that, Cass. You're doing so much work, and I could never have done this without you."

She didn't respond at first. Once again, I'd managed to yank my foot up to my mouth. Writing words instead of talking had always given me the advantage of being able to rip them up or cross them out before showing them to someone. But when words were spoken, they just rolled out, and sucking them back in was impossible.

"Well, I've got to make dinner for Dray," she said quietly.

"Cassie, please don't be upset. Everything will be fine."

She sighed. "Yeah. Bye."

Nix walked inside just as I hung up. "That is not a happy face," he said. "What's wrong?"

I put the phone down and picked up the package. It was light, and shaking it produced no sound. "I stupidly mentioned to Cassie that maybe we should have eloped, and it hurt her feelings. Don't know why I said it except we didn't have much time to plan this wedding out."

Nix walked over and put his arm around my waist and kissed my forehead. "The only thing I need at this wedding is you, and you can walk down that aisle in a paper bag, for all I care."

"Glad you're open to that concept. It's more likely than you'd imagine."

He tapped the package. "What's that? An early wedding gift?"

TESS OLIVER

"I have no idea what it is. It's addressed to me from someone in Burbank. I don't know anyone out there. Do you?"

He gave it some thought. "No one I can think of." He lifted it and put it near his ear. "It's not ticking, so I guess it's safe to open."

I stared at the package. "Jeez, now I'm not so sure. I hadn't even thought about something bad inside."

"There's nothing bad in there. It's light and quiet. And I'll be here to grab it if it's a snake."

I looked up at him. "Good to know." I peeled off the packing tape and the brown wrapper. The box was taped too. Someone had gone to great care to make sure whatever was inside was safely packaged. I cleared away some of the white packing peanuts. There was an envelope on top of a small tin box. The envelope had two names on the front— Scotlyn and Olivia. Just seeing my sister's name made my fingers tremble. Nix stood as silent as a statue behind me as I opened the envelope.

Dear Ms. James,

You don't know me, but some years ago I bought a few items at an estate sale. My main purchase was a small trunk that had various pieces of custom jewelry and other trinkets. The name James was carved into the top of the trunk. Inside the trunk was a small tin box. This is what I have mailed to you. I recently read of the upcoming nuptials of a Ms. Scotlyn James and Nix Pierce. As the name Scotlyn is so unique, I have mailed this box on the hunch that you are the Scotlyn to which it belongs. Inside, you will find a note to

182

explain more. I hope I have found the right person and best wishes for a happy marriage.

Sincerely,

Margaret Parker

I stared down at the silver tin box. It had small white daisies painted on it. I had never seen it before. I had no idea what was inside, but my limbs felt heavy and my head felt light. This box had belonged to my mom. I could sense it.

Nix placed his hand on my arm. "Maybe you should sit down."

It took me a second to process his suggestion. I reached inside and picked up the box. The tin was cold and smooth in my fingers as I walked over to the table and sat down. The newspaper with the article, the article that'd brought this box to my hands, sat in front of me.

It took some effort to pop the top open. Inside was a tiny note. I recognized my mom's handwriting, excessively curly and slightly hurried, and my throat tightened at the sight of it. The paper twitched in my shaky fingers. Nix pulled up a chair next to me, but he hadn't said a word. I unfolded the thin, yellowed from time, paper. There was a tiny vine of flowers printed on one side. "To my beautiful daughters, Scotlyn and Olivia, if I'm handing you this box then it must be your wedding day. I fashioned these two garters from the lace and beads on my wedding dress. I'm sure the dress itself will be too out of style by the time you girls get married, but I wanted you to have a part of it to wear on your special day. Your dad says I'm a sentimental nerd, but what does he know? Anyhow, my loves, I hope you like them."

Tears flowed down my cheeks as I reached in and lifted

out one of the garters. Ivory lace was neatly sewn onto a pink garter band and a row of iridescent beads ran along each border. The one I held had the letter S embroidered on the center with white thread. The second one was exactly the same but with the letter O embroidered on the center.

Nix took the garter carefully from my trembling hands. He scooted the chair back and got down on his knee. Gently, he slipped off my sandal. I stared down at him through tear-blurred eyes as he slid the garter up my leg.

I fingered the lace. "I can't believe this. I wonder when she made these." I lifted Olivia's out of the tin and pressed it to my cheek, hoping to catch a small whiff of my mom's wonderful scent on the lace. But too many years had passed.

"I'll wear this one too. Then I'll have a little of both of them there with me." I couldn't stop the tears.

Nix took my hand and we walked into the family room. He sat on the couch and I crawled into his lap. I couldn't take my eyes off the garter. I could see my mom's slim, long fingers pulling the thread through the lace. She'd probably been smiling and listening to rock and roll while she made it. She was always smiling. And she was always listening to rock and roll. And she was always thinking of Olivia and me. It was hard to believe that her gift had found its way back to me. "I will have to write Mrs. Parker a letter, to let her know just how much this means to me. She must be a wonderful person. She deserves a big thank you."

I rested my head against Nix's chest and he tightened his arms around me.

CHAPTER 27

Nix

Taylor came out of the house dressed in extremely short shorts and with her blouse tied up right beneath her breasts. It was the same way she'd dressed when she was a flirty seventeen-year-old trying her hardest to drive Clutch crazy. Which she had. But my stoic friend had behaved himself. Even though Taylor's parents had gone out of their way to separate her from Clutch, who they had ignorantly deemed not good enough for her, once she'd turned eighteen, Clutch gave up the fight. He was nuts about her, and they'd been together ever since. Until now.

I looked over at Scotlyn. "If Clutch asks, remember this was your idea."

"Coward," she muttered as Taylor opened the back door and slid inside.

"Hey, it's the newlyweds. Oh wait, I guess that would be the almost newlyweds." Taylor had a tendency to talk a lot and fast when she was nervous.

Scotlyn turned around. "You look adorable. I love that blouse."

"Thanks. I sewed it earlier this summer. And don't worry, Scottie, I started working on the dresses again. I figure I'm destined to be alone, and I need to be able to make my own living."

"That's silly. You won't be alone," Scotlyn said. "But you still need to make your own living. Independence is good for everyone, alone or not. And I'm not worried about the dresses."

"Phew, that's good to hear. Cassie seems a little tense every time she calls. I told her I just wasn't feeling it, you know? But my creativity surged back this morning. I mean to hell with Clutch." She paused. "He's not bringing anyone to this meet, is he, Nix?"

I peered up at her in the mirror. She bit her lip in worry, waiting for my response.

"I haven't talked to him for a few days, but I think he's just going to find a buyer for his Nova."

She relaxed back with a small grin. "Not that I care, but I was just wondering."

"Right," I said.

She took off her seatbelt and leaned forward. "I almost forgot— Cassie told me about the garter your mom made. We were both bawling like babies when she told me." She reached over and put her hand on Scotlyn's shoulder. "That is about the coolest thing in the world."

"I agree." Scotlyn squeezed her hand. Taylor never had a sister, and Scotlyn had lost hers. They'd formed an instant bond. Taylor looked up to Scotlyn like an older sister.

The extreme heat of summer tended to make the car meets extra crowded. As the sun dropped down, people migrated out from the air conditioning into the cool night air. Tonight, it seemed even nightfall wouldn't bring relief from the heat.

We climbed out of the car. Music from various speakers shot toward each other clashing in the middle. "Oh look, the crepe truck." Scotlyn pointed to a lime green food truck. "I've been dying to try one."

I raised a brow at her. "Really? Aren't they just undersized pancakes?"

"No, they are not." She held out her palm. "I didn't bring my purse. Taylor, are you up for some strawberry crepes?"

Taylor nodded but wasn't actually listening to the question. She stretched up as far as she could on her toes, no doubt searching for the big blond head.

"Taylor?" Scotlyn said again.

She dropped back down to flat feet. "Crepes sound great."

"You guys eat your flat-ironed pancakes. I'm going for a burger." I waited for them to disappear around the corner of the crepe truck, then I headed to the spot where Clutch usually parked. His Nova was sitting under a light, and Clutch's chair was next to it, empty. The guy at the next car, who I always saw at all the meets, but whose name I never knew, motioned across the lot. "Clutch just took a test drive in someone's Pontiac. He'll be right back, I'm sure."

"Thanks." I headed back toward the food trucks before the girls noticed me missing. I'd hoped to catch Clutch first to warn him that Taylor had come along with us. That was obviously not going to happen. I considered texting him but then decided to just let the evening take its natural course.

A familiar laugh caught my attention, and I peered over

187

some heads. Stormy was standing with a group of friends. She saw me and cast me an extremely icy and completely expected glare. I continued on to the burger truck.

The crepe truck was not the most popular food supplier at a vintage car meet, and Scotlyn and Taylor were already sitting and eating before I'd even reached the order window. I was trying to assess which way the night was going to go. The break-up had already stretched longer than I'd expected, but it just didn't seem possible that Clutch was going to give Taylor up.

I walked to the table with my burger. Scotlyn was licking her fingertip and picking up the stray powdered sugar from her paper plate. "You missed out, sweetie. The crepes were delicious."

"Those are dessert." I lifted my double cheeseburger from the wrapper. "This is dinner."

Scotlyn stared at it. "You know that does look tasty. By the way, and don't be mad."

I looked past my burger at her. "Uh oh. What?"

She tapped the side of her head. "Let me restart. I should lead with some good news. I think it's all good news, but you might not love the second part of what I'm going to tell you, especially with the way you're looking at that burger."

"My burger is getting cold, Scottie."

"Right." She looked at Taylor whose curiosity was also now piqued. "Cassie was having a problem getting someone to do the lighting since we're having the wedding late to avoid the August heat. We were afraid we'd have to stick flashlights in the bouquets."

"I think that would be cool," Taylor said, "in a creepy,

haunted wedding kind of way, I mean."

"Well, we won't need to. Nicky King wanted to thank Cassie for taking such great pictures of Finley's barn. He is going to have his stage crew string up the lights for the wedding. And the best part is, he's covering the cost."

No longer able to wait, I'd taken a big bite of burger while she talked. "Free is good," I said after swallowing.

"Really?" Scotlyn asked. "That's the exciting part? Nicky King's roadies are going to decorate our wedding set."

"Yeah, that's cool. I'm just saying free is good. But what about the part where I get mad?"

"About that—" She looked at my burger. "Since Finley got us the awesome location for our wedding, and I can soften this news again with the words 'for free', I told her we didn't need any beef or pork for the wedding dinner. After all, Some Pig is on the invite list. In fact, we're going Mediterranean vegetarian."

My mouth dropped. "We're eating lettuce and carrots for our wedding dinner?"

"Jeez, you are spending way too much time with Dray. It will be delicious, you'll see."

I took an extra large bite of my burger.

She leaned over and kissed my cheek. "To make up for it, I'll let you call all the shots on our wedding night." She winked at me.

"Hmm, well that does make up for the lack of meat. I'm just hoping a vegetarian wedding dinner will give me enough strength to last the wedding night."

Taylor got up. "All righty, this conversation is starting to get awkward. I'm going to wander around."

Scotlyn got up. "I'll come with you."

Taylor grinned at her. "Scottie, I'm not going to go throw myself at his feet and beg for forgiveness."

"No, I wouldn't expect that. It's just he doesn't know you're here yet."

I wadded up the greasy wrapper and got up from the bench. "Let's all go surprise him. I'll tell him about the vegetarian dinner for a double whammy."

The three of us headed toward the corner where Clutch's Nova was parked. Halfway there, Taylor stopped. "Nevermind. I don't want to see him. It's just going to make me upset again. He'll probably be all grumpy and cold and I don't think I can take that." She looked at Scotlyn. "And then I always cry. Why do I have to always fucking cry, and he just stands there with this stony statue expression while my nose gets red and runny."

Scotlyn glanced my way and took hold of her arm. "I know all about that, believe me. If you don't want to see him, we can wander around and look at cars."

I waved at them. "See you later then." I kept going, but their small footsteps seemed to be following. I looked back over my shoulder. Scotlyn shrugged. Apparently, Taylor had decided to head toward Clutch after all.

I was fifty feet from his Nova. The girls had hung back a good ten feet. Stormy was pressed against Clutch, and he was leaning against his Nova, bracing his hands on the edge of the car. There was no smile on his face. In fact, he looked stiff and a little confused. I spun around and tried to turn the girls back, but it was too late. Taylor's face paled as she shoved past me and stepped into a clearing. It took Clutch only a second to spot her standing there with her shoulders rigid and her bottom lip trembling. Scotlyn tried to take her hand, but she yanked it away.

Clutch slid out and away from Stormy. He looked as shocked as Taylor. Stormy sneered at me and marched away.

"Look, Taylor, that girl used to work for me. She's really forward. I have had her come on to me like that, too."

Scotlyn's eyes widened as she looked over Taylor's head at me. "What? You never mentioned that."

"Because there was no need to. I told her no and that was that. It's one of the reasons I fired her. She's— she's too much."

Clutch walked reluctantly toward us, but Taylor tore off through the crowd. Scotlyn huffed at both of us and then followed her.

Clutch reached me. "What the hell, *friend*? You could have let me know she was coming."

"I tried to, but you were off on some test drive."

He looked around to see where Stormy had slithered off to. She was gone. "Man, that chick comes on strong."

"Yeah, she does."

"Do you think Taylor was pissed?"

Sometimes his lack of judging emotions, especially when it came to Taylor, stunned me. "Hmm, let's recap. You were leaning against your car, and a scantily dressed girl was pressed up against you."

"I didn't even touch her," Clutch said in his defense.

191

"Don't think that matters, do you?"

He combed his fingers through his hair and seemed to be considering the incident. "You know what? Fuck it. She just got a taste of her own medicine."

"Yeah, I guess that's one way to look at it. I'll hang with you a little while and then head out. I'm pretty sure Scotlyn and Taylor aren't going to want to hang around here long tonight."

We went over to his fold-out chairs and sat down. I could tell the whole thing had him more shaken than he wanted to let on. We sat there for a long time just watching people pass. Then he looked over at me.

"It was a hell of a lot easier when it was just you, me and Dray, partying and picking up on girls for one nighters," Clutch said.

"Easier, but not better, dude, and you know it as well as I do."

He stretched out his massive legs and slumped back against the chair. "Shit, don't know when we lost control of things, but we sure as hell did."

I joined him in a slump. "I know exactly when it happened for you, my normally uber-confident friend."

He dropped his face my direction. "You do?"

"Yep. We were sitting in these same damn chairs, which by the way it's about time you replace them. This one is so frayed it is cutting into my ass. Anyhow, we were sitting in these chairs and a seventeen-year-old Taylor was sashaying through a maze of cars wearing just her bright smile and an extremely short sundress. You stiffened next to me as if you'd been turned to cement. And just seconds before she reached us you said—"

He finished for me. "—that sweet little piece of trouble drives me fucking nuts."

"Yep, that's when it happened for you." I glanced over at him. "And for me, it was a picture getting stuck on my shoe."

CHAPTER 28

Scotlyn

Thanks mostly to Cassie's fortitude and slightly militant persistence, everything was in place for the wedding. I had no idea how I'd ever repay her for her help, and I was sure I wouldn't be nearly as effective of a wedding planner for her, if she and Dray decided to marry. Taylor's dresses were so beautiful that we all modeled them around Finley's room for half an hour and then fell into a tearful huddle.

Taylor and Clutch still had not made up, but Nix assured me they would get back together. Occasionally, at work, Clutch would casually ask me if I'd talked to Taylor, and I was always happy to relay anything that was happening in her life. I told him that he would be blown away by the dresses she was designing and sewing. That always produced a proud smile that he tried hard not to let me see.

At Nicky King's invitation, we'd all arrived at the estate on the Thursday before the wedding. I could hardly believe that Nix and I would be married in two days. I couldn't have been happier.

Finley had set Cassie and me up in a room. Taylor was bunking with her and Some Pig. The guys had their own rooms down the hall. It was sort of nice to have a little space between us and the men for a few days. They'd all spent the morning in the gym with Jude and Cole, Finley's brothers. Eden, Finley's best friend and Jude's girlfriend and the sister to the two flower girls, was living in the pool house with Jude. Her family was driving down from up north where they lived and worked. The wedding rehearsal was planned for Friday, once everyone had arrived. Nicky King had a friend who had one of those online minister certificates, and he was all set to marry us.

Sunset at the estate was beautiful, and we women, including Cole's new girlfriend, Veronica, a kindergarten teacher and super sweet person, had decided to make frothy, fruity drinks and sit out by the pool. The men had decided some of Nicky's quality porn in the estate's private theater was more to their liking. I put the finishing touches on my wedding vows and slid on my sandals. Nix was just coming out of their bedroom as I stepped into the hallway. We'd hardly seen each other all day.

He smiled and made a point of looking down the length of me. He trapped me between him and the hallway wall by bracing a hand on each side of my head. "You are wearing my favorite sundress, and I'm not even going to be there. Maybe I should join you girls instead."

"Nope, girls only. Like the ice chest."

"Nicky King is hanging out with you."

"Well, yeah, he's Nicky King." I hopped on my tiptoes and kissed him.

One of his hands dropped down to my leg, and he slid it up along my thigh and beneath my dress. "So, my angel dropped from heaven, are you ready for this?"

I fingered the black stubble on his chin. "I am." I chuckled. "Cassie might need a Valium, but I'm ready."

He smiled, it was a smile I knew in my sleep, in my dreams. It was a smile that still made my knees weak. "Dray is pretty amped up too. Wonder how they'll be on their wedding day."

"How's Clutch doing?"

"Being in the same house, even a house the size of a small city, with Taylor has him a little on edge. But something tells me the wedding is going to bring them back together. I hope. He's kind of bumbling around like a giant airhead, which is not like him."

"Poor guy. When he sees the dresses Taylor made, he'll be so impressed."

Footsteps and tiny hooves sounded on the stairs. Finley and Some Pig appeared on the top step, both breathing hard as if they'd just run a race.

"Some Pig, dude," Nix laughed, "you need to lay off those nachos."

"We just came from where they are setting up for the wedding. The lights are done. It's still not dark out but come see."

Nix and I followed her through the house. It was easy to get lost in it. Cassie and Taylor stopped what they were doing in the kitchen to go with us. A crew of four guys were just folding up ladders and putting away tools. There were dozens of light strings stretching from gleaming white posts to the massive, ornate gazebo in the center of the lush lawn area. A temporary stage had been constructed near the gazebo. Nicky waved to us as we reached the wedding area. He was holding a remote.

"Ready?" he called.

Finley gave him a thumbs up and he pressed his finger down on the remote. Thousands of tiny gold lights flickered on, creating a carpet of twinkling stars across the yard. My hand flew to my mouth. I raced over to Nicky and gave him a hug. "It's like a fairytale," I cried. "How can I ever thank you?"

"My pleasure, love," he said.

The others had gathered now under the lights. Cassie stared up and turned around as if she was star gazing. "It's perfect." She stopped spinning and smiled at me. "This is going to be awesome."

I ran over to her and threw my arms around her. "I can't even believe this is happening. But none of it would have come together without you, Cass."

CHAPTER 29

Nix

Nicky King's porn selection had been organized alphabetically, but like little kids in a candy shop, we couldn't decide. Since I was the groom to be, the task fell to me. I picked one that looked interesting. Rett and Cole poured beers at the small bar at the back of the theater. Jude took care of the technical stuff. The King theater had soft leather chairs, an incredible sound system and a screen that rivaled a real movie theater in size.

Clutch stood up front with his beer mug. "To my best friend, Nix. May your marriage be filled with happiness, good fortune and lots of smokin' hot sex."

"Here, here." Everyone raised their mugs.

Clutch paused. "But, in all seriousness, buddy, I wish you the best. I love you, bro."

I raised my beer to him again. "Love you too."

Dray got up from his seat. "All right, now it's time for a toast from his real best friend, not his alternative best bud."

Clutch laughed and came to sit next to me. "This should give you a preview of what the best man's toast is going to be like." Having two best friends made the best man thing

TESS OLIVER

a sticky subject, but Clutch had told me more than once that he was glad to be walking Scotlyn down the aisle. It had been a hard choice. I loved them both. But I knew Dray would have been hurt the most if I hadn't picked him.

Dray was already done with his first beer. He lifted his glass and stared at it. "Wait, bartenders, can I get another?"

Rett came up front with another beer.

Dray poured it into his glass. "To my best friend, Nix. Don't know why you thought this was wise, and now, of course, you've got Cassie thinking about weddings and I may never forgive you for that, but—" He raised his glass. "I wish you happiness, bro, you deserve it. And Scotlyn is amazing."

Jude got the movie up and running and we settled in to watch.

The actors got right to action. "Boy, this one has an intriguing plot," Dray said. "Good choice."

"Thank you, the cover looked thought provoking," I said. "And I must say this one is making my manhood throb and glisten." All heads turned toward me.

"Trying out some new vocabulary?" Clutch asked.

"Thought I'd give it a whirl. Do you like it?"

"No. Now shut up. We're missing the dialogue."

He knuckled me on the shoulder. "Dude, can't believe you're getting hitched."

"Yeah, me neither. You know, for the first few years after high school, it seemed like all three of us were in a freefall. But you know what they say?"

"What's that?" Clutch asked.

200

"The best way to stop a freefall is by landing on your feet."

Dray leaned over. "Who says that?"

"Don't know," I said. "Me, I guess. But we all landed on our feet, and I think that's pretty cool."

"Here, here." Dray and Clutch lifted their beers with mine.

The theater doors opened and Nicky King walked down the aisle. He stood in the front and stared up at the screen. "I dated the blonde in this movie for a few weeks."

"You make a son proud, Dad," Cole called to him.

Nicky looked around. "Just thought I'd let all you blokes know that the girls finished their fruity drinks and stripped down to their bras and panties to jump in the pool. I came in here because Finley made me leave."

Rett was the first one up. "I already know how this ends, so I think I'll head out to the pool."

The rest of us left a trail of flames behind us in our rush to get out to the pool. We all crammed into the elevator that would take us to the main floor. "Do you think they'll be pissed if we join them?" Dray asked.

"Probably," Clutch said.

"Yeah, probably," Jude said.

The elevator door opened and a comedy scene followed with six big shouldered guys trying to squeeze out all at once. Jude led the way, and we thundered through the house and out to the pool area.

The girls shrieked and put on a good show of shock as we stripped down to our underwear and jumped into the water.

Scotlyn was sitting on the small island in the center of the lake-sized pool. I gripped the edge of the island as she smiled down at me. "What happened to porn night in the theater?"

"There was better stuff happening out here." I looked over to the deep end. Clutch was sitting on the edge of the pool next to Taylor. "Hey, looks like this might be it."

Scotlyn glanced over her shoulder. "I hope so. Poor Taylor is just not herself without him." She took my hand. "I get kind of lost without my soul mate too." She slid into the water and snuggled against me.

"Who is up for some volleyball in the pool?" Cole called.

"What do you think?" I asked.

"Sure. I just hope my panties stay on when I'm jumping up and down."

"Yeah, that's what I'm hoping too."

Taylor's wild laugh echoed through the pool area. Clutch had her up and over his shoulder. Water dripped off both of them as he passed us by. Taylor lifted her head and smiled our direction. "Make-up sex," she giggled.

I looked at Scotlyn. "See, that is the part I just love about her," she said.

"Hey, leave a fucking necktie on the door," Dray called to him. "Otherwise, I can't promise that I won't be barging in on you."

Clutch didn't respond, but picked up a towel on his way past the lounges. Taylor laughed all the way to the house.

Chapter 30

Scotlyn

Lennon Marley, the man who was going to marry us, had long dreadlocks, a Hawaiian shirt, sandals and either he was wearing aftershave that smelled like weed or he'd smoked a lot of joints on the way to the wedding. My parents would have loved him. After meeting him, Nix whispered in my ear, "Not sure if we'll be legally married, but this should be fun".

Finley's room had been transformed into a beauty parlor, dressing room combination. Fortunately, the room was bigger than Nana's entire house. Some Pig's snout twitched as we scurried around him with flat irons waving in the air like swords on a pirate ship. A slightly intoxicating aroma of nail polish, perfume and the citrusy mimosas Finley had had the chef whip up for us circled around the room making me feel even more heady.

Cassie, who normally dressed in somber colors and black, floated over in her bridesmaid dress. "Cassie, that pink color is gorgeous on you."

She glanced down at the perky dress and then peered up at me through her large, black rimmed glasses. She'd decided to leave her contacts out until the last minute. They always irritated her, and she much preferred her glasses. But, as the official wedding photographer, the contacts made things easier. "I do feel sort of girly for a change. I kind of like it. Maybe I'll add a few spring colors to my wardrobe." She reached up to help me take the rollers from my hair. Taylor had insisted the dress and flower wreath begged for curls and that a curling iron just wouldn't do the job right. "I took the sweetest picture of Sophie and Janie helping Some Pig put on his little tux shirt. They haven't left that pig alone all day, but he doesn't seem to mind. In fact, he seems to be enjoying the attention."

"My pig wants to be a little girl's doll in the next life," Finley said. "Sophie and Janie, why don't you walk Some Pig out to the wedding so he can find a seat." The girls looked like the princesses they dreamed of as they raced out in a flurry of pink satin. Some Pig trotted proudly behind in his custom made tuxedo shirt.

Finley started with the curlers on the back. "Guests are arriving downstairs. My dad is entertaining them all with the sordid, tabloid worthy details of his life." She laughed. "I swear I saw Nix's sister cover her son's ears." She gathered up an armload of curlers and stepped in front of me. "And Nix looks beyond beautiful in his tux. He also looks a little nervous, which is something I've never seen. It's really cute."

Taylor carried over the flower wreath and pinned it on my head. "That florist did an awesome job with the flowers. Everything looks beautiful."

"I'll have to make sure to let people know about her. She's trying hard to break into the business, and she deserves to break in big." I smiled at Cassie. "Maybe when

Cass opens up her wedding planning company, she can use her as a florist."

Cassie shook her head. "One wedding in a lifetime is more than enough."

"Oh, but I'm hoping you'll plan mine someday," Taylor said.

"Well, maybe yours but that's it."

"Oh, poo," Finley said.

"And, maybe yours. It will be a lot of fun because I would imagine the budget would be off the charts. Oh my gosh, we could have you and Rett helicopter in together."

Finley laughed. "Don't know about a helicopter, but wouldn't Rett look hot riding in on a big black horse?"

"Rett could shuffle in on a scooter and still look hot," Taylor laughed.

"That boy does know how to light up a room," I said.

"Enough about Rett, your own groom is waiting out there." Cassie shifted the wreath a tiny bit to the left. "I can tell you, Scottie, he is so damn thrilled to be marrying you."

The truth was, I was excited about this wedding mostly because I couldn't wait just to be alone with Nix, in his arms reminiscing and laughing about the day. "Cass, did you see where I left my glass, I think I could use another sip." I steadied my hands by holding them together. "I think the butterflies are really starting to jump now."

"It's on the dresser. I'll get it." She stopped and took hold of my hands first. "You're supposed to be nervous. And you look incredible."

She hurried away and came back with the drink and the

tin box with the garters. "I think it's time to put these on. You don't want to forget them." She lifted her finger and waved it at me. "And no tears. The mascara is waterproof, but you don't want streaks down your cheeks."

I took hold of the box and, of course, tears threatened immediately. I took a sip of the drink and then sucked in a deep breath to settle myself down. I sat on the edge of Finley's bed and Cassie, Taylor and Finley sat down with me. My fingers trembled as I opened the tin box.

"Do you think I should wear my sister's too?"

"What does your heart tell you to do?" Finley asked.

"It will be like having a tiny piece of Olivia with me up there at the altar."

Cassie put her hand on my arm. "Then wear it."

I lifted both garters out of the box. The girls leaned in to get a better look at them. "They are lovely," Finley said. "What a cool mom."

"She was the best. And she would have loved this dress," I smiled at Taylor. "Thank you so much."

"Thank you for letting me design the wedding dresses."

Finley glanced over at her. "You need to get some business cards made up. I think there are going to be people asking for it after tonight."

"I'm glad you and Clutch made up before the wedding," Cassie said. "I would have hated to take pictures of Clutch glowering down at the camera. He was such a grump while you two were apart."

"Yeah, I think the little separation ended up being harder on him than on me."

I took a deep breath. "Taylor, can you help put these on. I don't want to crinkle my dress."

She leaned down and slid the garters over my foot. I adjusted them high on my thigh and admired my mom's loving handiwork. Music started out in the yard. There was a knock on the door.

Eden poked her head inside. "We're ready." She pushed inside. "Scotlyn, you are breathtaking."

I smiled. "I think we're ready. Group hug everyone, and no smearing makeup on my dress."

"Yes, I still have to turn it in as homework," Taylor quipped.

We hugged and laughed. I took a deep breath. Cassie led the way. The bouquets were waiting for us on the kitchen counter. Eden handed each of her little sisters, who were giggling wildly with nerves, a basket with rose petals. "Now remember, just one petal at a time."

Finley shook her head. "Jeez, I hope Some Pig can control himself when he sees rose petals fluttering down to the ground. They're like candy to him."

"I think it would be adorable and a quick way to clean up," I said. We walked out through the pool area and down the long path of tall boxwood shrubs. On the other side, Nicky King, and the musicians who were backing him up, began to play his famous love song, "Angel's Tears". I bit my lip to keep back the tears and hold myself together. My family wasn't sitting on the other side of the shrubs, but the people who mattered most to me were there, waiting. And Nix.

Cassie winked back at me before she stepped around

the shrubs to meet Dray. Eden, who was helping, motioned me forward, and I stepped around the boxwoods. Everyone stood and my fingers shook as I tightened them around my bouquet. Thousands of lights twinkled like stars and a warm California breeze drifted across the lawn. Clutch had left his place up at the altar. His confident smile calmed me some. He held out his arm, and I wrapped my hand around it. "You look beautiful, Scottie," he said quietly. "You ready?"

"I am."

We walked forward. Some Pig had, as Finley predicted, jumped off his chair, and he trotted ahead of us vacuuming up the rose petals as he went. Janie ran out and tried to shoo him away, but he was a determined pig. We reached the bottom of the altar, which was just the landing on the steps of the gazebo. The music had gotten Lilly Belle's attention, and she mooed in the distance. A wave of quiet laughter rolled through the guests.

Clutch leaned down and gave me a kiss on the cheek, and as he moved back to his spot, I got my first real glimpse of Nix. He looked dashing and perfect in his tux. The way he looked at me made my throat ache. There had been a time in my life when I was certain I would never be happy again. Thank goodness I was so wrong.

CHAPTER 31

Nix

"I memorized my vows, but seeing you in that dress is making it hard to remember my own name." The guests laughed and it gave me a second to catch my breath. Scotlyn's smile spurred me on, and I held her hands in mine. "Three years ago, I found your picture at a car meet. It was stuck on the toe of my shoe." More laughter, including Scotlyn's. "A girl with amazing blue eyes and incredible lips stared up at me from that picture, and she seemed to be saying, please come find me. Dray laughed when I told him that I'd found a picture of my future wife." Scotlyn's eyes watered, and I squeezed her hands. "From the second you walked into my life, you captured my heart and my soul. I am yours...completely. I will try hard not to disappoint you, and I'll never complain when you use my shirt like a kleenex during a sad movie." Scotlyn laughed through her tears. I paused for a second to lift her hand and kiss it. "Scotlyn James, I will love, protect and worship you forever."

Lennon Marley, who'd shed his bright Hawaiian shirt for a tame white one, looked at Scotlyn. "Scotlyn, your vows."

Scotlyn took a breath. "When I couldn't speak, you were

the first person to hear me. From the moment I met you, I could feel you listening to me with your heart, and I will never forget that. Alexander Nix Pierce, thank you for helping me find my voice. Your kisses turn my knees to jelly. Your smile makes my head spin. And your love and friendship have filled the hole in my heart. I will love you forever. And I promise to remember to bring the box of kleenex when we sit down to a sad movie."

I reached for her before Mr. Marley had the words 'kiss the bride' out of his mouth. Dray and Rett howled loudly and cheers went up as I kissed my bride.

***

After a long photo session with an extremely particular photographer, and three clownish groomsmen, who were like anxious kids waiting to get to the open bar, Scotlyn and I managed to get to our first dance. Nicky King was in full rock star mode singing one of Scotlyn's favorites, "Run to You" as I pulled her into my arms. I kissed her again. "O.K., there is cool, and there is having Nicky King sing at your wedding cool."

"Hmm, and I was just thinking there is cool, and there is standing in Nix Pierce's arms cool."

"Now I feel like a heel."

She laughed. "Nope, you're just honest. That's one of the things I love most about you."

"One of the things?"

She fingered the rose on my lapel. "Well, there are many other things, but some aren't appropriate to list on a dance floor with other people. I'll tell you about them later. When we're alone."

I held her closer. "Alone, why does that word sounds so delicious right now?"

"Because you're antsy about getting me out of this dress."

"I do love the dress, but yes, my thoughts are mostly about taking it off."

We kissed and danced and laughed for the rest of the night.

When it came time for Scotlyn to throw the bouquet, the unmarried women, including the two flower girls, gathered around to catch it. Some Pig stood nearby, obviously deciding it would be as delicious as the rose petals. Dray, Clutch, Rett and I stood in the back, deciding that was where we'd get the best view. A cluster of pink satin bridesmaid dresses rustled in the center of the catch zone.

The bouquet went sailing over the heads of the all the women. Clutch's high school football instincts surfaced and he reached up and caught it. His eyes went wide and he stared at the flowers as if he'd caught a bouquet of live snakes. As if he was playing a game of Hot Potato, he tossed it straight over to Cassie.

She held it up triumphantly. Taylor scowled at Clutch.

Dray knuckled him hard on the arm. "You did that on purpose."

"No, I just threw it, and it happened to go straight to Cassie." He grinned down at Dray. "Almost as if it was supposed to be."

Dray looked at me. "Do you fucking believe this? I'm not going to hear the end of it now." As he ranted on, the

211

bouquet smacked his face and dropped to the ground. Cassie was staring at him with her hands on her hips.

Dray picked it up. "I'm just kidding, sweetie pie." He walked over to Cassie and pulled her into his arms, but still managed a snarly glance at Clutch.

Scotlyn came up next to me and took my arm as the band started up again. "I think this is our song," she said.

"I didn't know we had a song."

"We do now." She stopped and put her arms around my neck. "I am completely and deliriously happy, Nix Pierce."

"Me too, Scotlyn James Pierce." My arms went around her and we kissed.

MORE CUSTOM CULTURE BOOKS

Freefall (Custom Culture #1)

Clutch (Custom Culture #2)

Dray (Custom Culture #3)

Rett (Custom Culutre #4)

Read more about Finley, Eden, Jude and Cole in **Strangely Normal**.

Made in the USA
San Bernardino, CA
05 February 2017